THE
PRACTICE
BOYFRIEND

THE
PRACTICE
BOYFRIEND

CHRISTINA BENJAMIN

CROWN ATLANTIC
PUBLISHING

Copyright © 2017 by Christina Benjamin
All rights reserved.
Published in the United States by Crown Atlantic Publishing

ISBN 978-1542441094

Text set in Adobe Garamond

Version 1.1
Printed in the United States of America
First edition paperback printed, January 2017

To all the boys I've loved before.

CHAPTER

1

The ping of her online chat window startled Hannah Stark from her studies. She quickly muted her laptop and pulled up the conversation—rolling her eyes when she saw who it was from.

techE: Hey I thought you were at school???

Str8-A: I am. Stalk much?

techE: Just wondering what my little genius is doing online.

Str8-A: Research. The internet is a wondrous thing. You should check it out.

techE: Internet's got nothing on me. But for real, what's up? You ditching class?

Str8-A: No If you must know I'm in the library working on my grad speech, but it's hopeless. Nothing I write is remotely relatable.

techE: What do your friends say?

Str8-A: I have no friends, remember?
techE: Why don't you do something about that???
Str8-A: Yeah in the 4 weeks of school left?
techE: It's never too late to start. You can do anything you set your mind to.
Str8-A: Thanks for the pep talk, Dad. Now scram. You're making me look lame.

Hannah scanned the stuffy library of her overly priced prep school. Luckily no one seemed to notice she'd been chatting online with her dad. *But that was the problem, wasn't it?* No one ever noticed her. Case in point—why she had no friends and had spent the first half of her lunch period chatting with her tech-geek dad who routinely hacked her computer to *check* for viruses. Basically he was spying on her. But he couldn't help it. It was sort of his job being in the biz and all.

Hannah stretched her stiff muscles before deleting another perfectly good graduation speech. There was one month of school left and she was already done—coasting on autopilot. She was first in her class, graduating with honors and her associate degree. The last thing she had to do was write the speech she'd give as the class valedictorian. But for some reason that task eluded her.

The more YouTube videos she watched of glossy-eyed seniors giving stellar speeches that ended in an eruption of applause the more Hannah realized she'd finally found something that her academic mind couldn't solve. The legendary valedictorians that had gone before her all had something Hannah didn't—a life!

She groaned and massaged her temples in frustration before opening a blank word document. She never had trouble writing. It was her specialty. Even now, she knew her writing wasn't really the problem. The problem was that she couldn't make herself believe anything she wrote. She couldn't relate to her classmates. She never had, and it seemed absurd that suddenly they'd want to hear anything she might have to say regarding fond memories and bright futures. She didn't make any with them.

Sadly, Hannah hadn't really made any memories in high school at all—outside of her education, of course. But no one wanted to hear about her math medals or writing awards. They didn't care that she was the youngest student to ever be accepted into Brown's business school. They didn't care that she'd been offered full ride scholarships to play tennis at six schools. They wanted to be reminded of the good times they'd shared and how their bonds formed at Stanton Prep had molded them into strong individuals ready to take on the world. *But how could she say all those things when she didn't believe them herself?*

She felt like a liar talking about carefree moments and wild memories that led to the precipice of their brave new future. Her classmates all knew she was a fraud on that front. She'd never gotten to know them. She'd been afraid to let them look too deep.

The more Hannah tried to force herself to come up with something to say, the more anxious she felt. *How had she let her entire high school career pass her by?* That was just it. She looked at high school as a career. She'd forgotten to be a teenager, to fall in love, get her heart broken, forge friendships, share adventures, make poor choices, then learn from them, cherishing those bonds and memories forever.

The tightness in Hannah's throat told her tears were coming. *This was it. She'd finally lost.* School had always been a competition to Hannah. Having the best grades, the highest test scores, an undefeated tennis title, the most acceptance letters, beating everyone out for the coveted valedictorian title. She'd done it all. But the entire time, she was always looking over her shoulder, waiting for someone or something to best her and snatch away her perfect record. The fact that it was something as simple as not indulging her adolescence that was her undoing made Hannah's blood boil.

Her father's encouraging words replayed in her mind. Maybe it wasn't too late to start. She made up her mind. There was no way she was going to lose now. She'd given up all those foolish teenage experiences so she could be the best. *How was it fair that what she'd given up to achieve perfection now made her feel like she was somehow incomplete?*

Hannah straightened her spine and slammed her laptop shut. She took a deep breath. She would not let this stupid speech unnerve her. There was no reason she couldn't have it all. *Who said she couldn't be studious and popular?* She would resort back to her tried and true techniques for success—studying and practice.

How hard could it be to fit in? To be an average teenager? She'd never tried, but she had four weeks to cram in an entire high school social life. Hannah's father was right. If anyone could achieve it, Hannah knew it would be her. She was determined and when she set her mind on a goal, she always achieved it.

CHAPTER
2

STEP 1: IMMERSION

Hannah reasoned she just needed to immerse herself into a clique, study them and then join in. Maybe she could even handle a different clique each week? She scanned the quad deciding where to start. It was lunch this period and the lush green grounds of Stanton Prep were dotted with clusters of students enjoying the thawed spring weather. There were the jocks, freaks, geeks, flunkies, and of course, on the bridge that overlooked the campus, were the Goldens.

The Goldens were the popular kids. Someone at Stanton Prep coined the term long ago, donning all the trust fund brats, socialites, and celebrity offspring as the proverbial *golden* children. Born with more than a silver spoon in their mouth, these social climbers made the rules at Stanton.

Everyone wanted to be, date, or kill one of the Goldens. Knowing exactly where they'd be at this hour, Hannah zeroed in on them. They always held court on the bridge at lunch.

Everyone passed under it each day to enter and exit their campus, giving the Goldens the perfect view of their kingdom.

Hannah heard laughter coming from what her fellow classmates snidely referred to as the Golden Gate Bridge. She gazed studiously at the bright clothing and shiny hair peppering the stone bridge. That's where she would focus. The Goldens would be her Everest. If she could crack them she could gain access to any clique in the school.

Game on.

STEP 2: RECON

Hannah picked up her bagged lunch and moved closer to the bridge, settling directly below a cluster of three gorgeous senior girls. Savannah Huxley, Madison Carmichael and Blakely Anderson. They were all yammering on excitedly about something. Hannah silently chewed her PB&J listening intently.

"Madi . . . really? I think you can do better than Vera Wang," Blakely scoffed.

"What's wrong with Vera?"

"Nothing if you don't mind looking outdated."

Madison's perfectly glossed lips parted in shock. "Vera is classic!"

"Yeah, classic last year maybe."

Savannah piped up. "She's right, Madi. You wore Vera last year."

"But she's a close friend of Daddy's. I feel bad wearing someone else."

"This is the *last* Cohl ball. It's the culmination of our

high school reign. Our dresses need to be perfection," Savannah added. "This is how we will be remembered."

Harrison Cohl's masked ball! That was it. That was Hannah's ticket to high school social success. Harrison Cohl was one of the Goldens. Okay, more like *the* Golden. His parents, Alastair and Evelyn Cohl, were powerful politicians. They'd divorced over an alleged affair when he was a child but still worked together, each holding power positions in Boston's governing party. The Cohl's practically owned the state—a title their sons were happy to tout. And with a political safety net like that, the Cohl boys got away with everything. Including throwing hedonistic parties full of underage drinking, sex and debauchery.

The Cohl boys were legends at Stanton Prep. They basically built the Golden dynasty. *And their famous crown jewel?* Their not-so-secret, secret masked balls. They were held at a different location every year at the end of the semester. And you couldn't gain access unless you were given a coveted key. Of course Hannah had never been invited. She was pretty certain that the Goldens didn't even know she existed. Harrison Cohl certainly didn't. He was the youngest of the five Cohl boys and he would be graduating with Hannah in a few weeks. But not before throwing one last legendary party.

If Hannah could get an invite to the ball she would have no trouble making wild, carefree memories with her classmates. She reined in her excitement and focused back on the bickering girls.

"I'm going to be photographed more than a Kardashian when I show up on Harrison's arm," Blakely mussed.

"Not if I beat you to him!" Savannah sneered.

"Oh please, like either of you have a chance?"

"And you do, Madi?"

"I didn't say I did. But you know Harrison always goes dateless so he can play his games. It's half the fun of wearing a mask. Never knowing who's with who . . . the allure of bedding a stranger . . . it's all so romantic," Madison sighed.

"Oh god, Madi, give it a rest. It's not like you're going to meet prince charming. Besides, everyone knows you've slept with the whole senior class by now so no one will be new to you," Blakely retorted.

Savannah laughed, but Madison just smiled. "I guess I'm just a hopeless romantic. And how else is a princess to find her prince without trying them all?"

The three girls laughed.

"But seriously, I hope there'll be some new blood at this ball," Blakely whined.

"Well we know who won't be there," Savannah smirked,

Hannah followed Savannah's line of sight to the slouched figure that strolled under the Golden Gate with his hands stuffed in the pockets of his jeans. His dark, shaggy locks fell like curtains over his face as if trying to hide his identity, but it was no use. Even if he wore a mask everyone would know Cody Matthews.

"Kill anyone today, Cody?" Blakely called.

Cody flipped her off without looking behind him.

Hannah shook her head at Blakely's cruelty. It was true that Cody's girlfriend died when he crashed his car. He'd been driving home from one of Harrison's parties. He was drunk and lost control of the vehicle, slamming into a tree. It was quite the scandal, but not just because of the DUI. That happened quite often at Stanton. But Cody's girlfriend, Elena, was pregnant. They were both Goldens, but had been dropped with alarming speed once the pregnancy rumor caught fire.

The snickering above called Hannah's attention back to the vicious girls on the bridge. She wondered how they could be so cruel to one of their own. How did they not see that they could fall just as quickly as Cody had under the right circumstances?

"I don't know what Elena ever saw in him," Savannah scowled.

"I do. Tall, dark and handsome," Madison quipped.

"And dangerous," Savannah added.

"That just makes him sexier," Madison purred.

"Well you can forget about it. Harrison would kill you if he sees you flirting with him. Besides, it's not like he'll be at the ball."

"I wouldn't be so sure," Blakely replied. "He still has his key from last year."

"Only because he was locked up in rehab. There's no way Harrison would honor his key."

"He'd have to. There's only two rules . . . a key gets you in, and your mask never comes off."

Hannah smiled to herself as a plan started to unravel in her mind.

CHAPTER

3

STEP 3: FORMULATE A HYPOTHESIS
(AKA: THE PLAN)

The more Hannah eavesdropped on the Goldens the more she realized that she didn't have enough time to infiltrate them and get an invite to the ball on her own. She only had four weeks and as she looked around at the other cliques on the lawn she realized they'd had four *years* and still hadn't found a way to climb the social ladder to high school royalty. That just meant she'd have to come up with a different strategy and it just so happened his name was Cody Matthews.

Facts: Cody possessed a key. And Cody owed Hannah.

After returning from rehab at the beginning of the school year, Cody was dangerously close to flunking out of Stanton. Being a tutor in every subject, Hannah was assigned to catch him up. He was still wrecked from losing everything he cared about—his girlfriend, his friends and even his spot on the basketball team—so getting him to focus had been a challenge. Hannah often wondered why Cody even came back to Stanton. It wasn't that she didn't think he was sharp. But there were plenty of good schools where his scandalous reputation might not have followed. When she asked him about it, he said he believed sins should be paid for.

She wasn't really sure why, but Hannah lost sleep over that comment. She knew Cody must wrestle more than a few nasty demons after what happened to his girlfriend, Elena. But to force himself to relive the pain every day by facing her friends at Stanton . . . it seemed too cruel.

Everyone blamed Cody for Elena's death. And the police report claimed it was his fault since he'd been driving drunk, so there really was no other argument. But still, it's not like Cody planned to kill Elena. He loved her. Hannah remembered how inseparable they'd been as a couple . . . Cody always doting on her, Elena cheering at his basketball games. It was sad that their love story ended in a drunken car crash. Hannah knew Cody wished he could take it back. Or at least that's what his quote in the paper implied. He'd said he'd do anything to take back what happened to Elena. But that didn't change the facts. Elena was dead and the students at Stanton Prep were happy to remind Cody that it was his fault.

Rumors swirled around Cody's return. Everyone thought he would be sent to prison, or juvee at least. But to return with little more than a stint in rehab and a suspended driver's license seemed like a slap in the face to Elena's friends. That's what the Goldens had become—Elena's champions. Even though they dropped her the moment they found out she was pregnant, after her death they'd adopted her back as their saint, if only to curse Cody further.

Harrison, who'd been Cody's best friend, was the coldest. As the basketball captain, it was his decision to kick Cody off the team. But strangely another rumor surfaced that it was Harrison's father's legal team that got Cody off with such a light sentence. It made no sense to Hannah, but then again she didn't try to understand the strange operating of the upper echelon.

With so much drama surrounding Cody, it wasn't any wonder why he couldn't focus on his studies. Hannah eventually took pity on him and passed him with C's on his make up exams so he could rejoin his classes. He'd graciously thanked her and in his own words had said, "I owe you one."

"Time to call in that favor, Cody," Hannah murmured to herself as she gathered her things and headed after him.

CHAPTER

4

STEP 4: EXECUTE THE PLAN

Hannah hadn't been able to locate Cody before the bell rang and classes reclaimed her for the remainder of the day. But she didn't worry . . . she plotted. She knew exactly where he'd be after school and headed straight there. Hannah smiled when she caught sight of him walking slowly down the road they shared. His backpack was slung over one shoulder and he had earbuds in, unable to hear her approach

They were on a secluded road, far away from the busy traffic near Stanton. Hannah had specifically waited in the parking lot for twenty-six minutes before starting her car and making the drive home. She passed Cody every day walking home from school. She knew this would be the best time to catch him—when he was alone, away from the prying eyes of the Goldens and gossips. Her plan needed to remain secret if it was going to work.

And just as she planned, Cody was now only about

a mile from his home, and half a mile from her own. She passed him and pulled onto the shoulder cutting him off. She could see his startled look in her rearview mirror. She took a deep breath. "You can do this, Hannah." After her pep talk she rolled down the window and waited for him to approach.

Cody stopped next to her navy Volvo and leaned down to look in at her. His brown hair fell over his golden-brown eyes, blocking the light that filtered in through the tree canopy above.

"Hey, Cody," Hannah said casually. "Do you want a ride home?"

"No thanks."

"I don't mind," Hannah persisted. "I mean, it's no trouble."

"You pass me walking home every day, Hannah. What made you stop today?"

The venom in Cody's voice sliced Hannah with guilt. He was right. She saw him every day and never offered him a ride before. "I . . . You're right. I'm sorry. That wasn't very kind of me. I'm usually so lost in thought I don't see what's right in front of me. But I'm trying to change that."

"Starting with me?" Cody asked suspiciously.

"Okay, fine. I need your help with something. Can you just get in the car?" Hannah barked impatiently.

"There it is," he said letting a smirk show.

"What?"

"Miss direct and to the point, Hannah Stark."

"Excuse me?"

"Oh, don't be ashamed of it. It's how you get your straight A's and stay above us, right? I actually admire it. It's refreshing compared to all the fake, two-faced snobs I deal with all day at Stanton."

"I don't think I'm above you!"

"Don't you?"

Hannah was silent. *Did she think she was above him?* She *was* planning to use him as a tool to get what she wanted. But she sort of was above him. Cody was barely passing, had no license, a dead girlfriend and a DUI. If he was going to insist on categorizing things then, yes, she was above him.

Cody was right and Hannah was on the verge of admitting that when he opened the backseat of her car and threw his bag in. He marched around to the passenger side and got in.

"Let's just get this show on the road, okay? I've got things to do."

Hannah looked over at his smug face. She was wrong to assume he was a shattered soul. He still held the air of a Golden—entitled, bothered, bored. This wasn't going to be as easy as she thought. But Hannah never backed down from a challenge and she wasn't about to start now.

CHAPTER
5

STEP 5: BLACKMAIL

Hannah put her car in drive and spoke clearly without moving her eyes from the road. "You owe me a favor, Cody, and I'm here to collect."

"What do you want?"

Straight to the point . . . good. He wasn't denying he owed her.

"I want your key to Harrison's ball."

Hannah kept her eyes on the road, but she could feel Cody staring at her. After a few moments he started to laugh.

"You're actually serious," he said between fits of laughter. "You want to go to a Cohl ball? *You?*"

Hannah gritted her teeth, hating his insulting tone. "You want to graduate, don't you?"

His laughter trailed off and she felt his eyes burning into her.

"If I divulge that you didn't *actually* pass your make up

exams you won't graduate."

"What do you want?" Cody asked flatly.

"I already told you. The key to Harrison's party."

"Why?"

"That's not important."

"Fine, but the key won't matter. You won't fit in."

"Then you'll tell me what I need to know so I *do* fit in."

Cody chuckled. "It's not something I can explain in one car ride home, Hannah."

"Fine, then I'll drive you to and from school until you've explained everything."

Cody scrubbed his face in frustration, realizing each time he opened his mouth he seemed to be making things worse for himself. "The inner workings of the people and things that happen at Harrison's parties wouldn't make any sense to you. You won't enjoy it."

"Why?"

"Because, you're not like us."

"You mean them," Hannah shot back. "You're not a Golden anymore." It was a low blow and she knew it, but Cody's cocky attitude was pissing her off.

"Yeah. Them." Cody replied quietly. He was silent for a while before he spoke again. "It's not a bad thing, Hannah. They're not good people. You don't want to be like them."

"You don't know what I want, Cody. You don't even know me."

"You're right. I don't know you. But I know Harrison and his crew. If you show up at the ball they'll pick you apart."

"Maybe I don't care."

"Why would you possibly want that abuse?"

"That's none of you're business. All you have to do is give

me the key and fill me in on what I need to know to fit in."

"Hannah, making you fit in isn't possible!"

"Then I guess you won't be graduating."

"Christ, Hannah! I'll give you my key, but I can't guarantee who the fickle pricks at Harrison's party will decide to stomp on."

"Fine. The key and your best effort."

"Fine!"

"So we have a deal?"

"Yes. It's a deal," Cody groaned.

Hannah smiled, looking at Cody for the first time. "Perfect. That wasn't so hard, was it?"

He shook his head. "I might have been wrong about you."

"What do you mean?"

"Extortion suits you. You're more like the Goldens than I thought."

CHAPTER

6

STEP 6: BEGIN TRAINING

The next morning Hannah pulled up outside Cody's massive house and beeped the horn. After five minutes of waiting she grew impatient, turned her car off and stormed up the stone steps.

"If he thinks he can blow me off he has another thing coming," Hannah muttered to herself. She pushed the pewter doorbell and listened to the pleasant chiming resonate through the house.

Cody lived in an impressive three-story New England style house. Everything was stone, white or covered with weathered cedar shakes. It was colossal compared to Hannah's modest two-story just up the road. Her family wasn't poor by normal standards, but compared to Cody's family and the rest of the Goldens, she was a pauper.

Hannah stepped back to look up at the windows, wondering which one was Cody's. She let out a low appreciative whistle taking in the beauty of his home up close. Hannah could admire the architecture, but she would never understand the need for such a huge home. From all the media coverage after his DUI, Hannah knew Cody didn't have any siblings and he lived in this home with only his father, Thomas Matthews, a corporate attorney for a ritzy hotel chain. According to the newspaper, Cody's mother, Tabitha, divorced after some family scandal and remarried when he was only six. She moved to New York with her new husband and had two children, whom Cody never met. The reporter's angle was that Cody had abandonment issues that led to his reckless ways.

All of the stories surrounding Cody's arrest whirled through Hannah's near photographic mind as she gazed at the palatial house. She shook her head. It didn't matter how regal the home looked, Cody would never escape his reputation in this town.

Hannah was about to press the doorbell again when she heard the locks tumbling. The door creaked open slightly and a short, thin man in a gray suit peered out at her. *Not Mr. Matthews.* Hannah knew his face from the news. *Maybe a butler? Did people really have those?*

"May I help you, miss?"

"Um, yes. I'm here to pick up Cody for school."

The man looked perplexed as he glanced at his watch. "It's 5 am."

"Yes, well I have tennis practice before school, so this is what time I leave."

The man blinked and opened the door wider. He made a sweeping gesture with his arm, ushering her inside. Hannah tried not to gawk at the lavish interior of Cody's home but the magnificent winding staircase and massive chandeliers dazzled her. When she realized her mouth hung open in awe she quickly snapped it shut and turned back to face the sharply dressed man.

"Cody and I made arrangements to ride to and from school together for the rest of the school year."

"Oh. I apologize, but Master Cody doesn't usually inform me of his plans. I'm afraid he may still be asleep. Would you like to me to wake him?"

Hannah sighed. "That's okay. I can do it myself. Can you point me to his room?"

The man's nervous eyes grew larger, but he nodded and led the way up the winding stairs. Hannah passed several maids dressed in pale gray uniforms, dusting or polishing the obscene amount of ornamental knickknacks. Hannah noticed how sterile the house felt as she followed the butler down the echoing marble hallways. Nearly everything in Cody's home was white. It reminded Hannah of an empty hospital. *How could anyone feel comfortable here?*

The butler's voice pulled her from her thoughts. "Master Cody's room is the last on the left," he said giving a curt bow before retreating back down the hall.

Strange. Hannah thought the butler would have at least walked her to the door. With how formal everything was it seemed like he should have announced her or something. *What if Cody wasn't even home? Would she just be left to wander the house and show herself out?*

Hannah checked her watch. 5:05. *Not good.* She was behind schedule. She would be late for tennis practice at this rate. Frustration drove her to march forward and knock on Cody's door.

No response.

"Jerk," she muttered to herself. It was day one and he was already pissing her off. But Hannah didn't get to where she was by giving up easily. She twisted the knob and barged into Cody's room.

It was pitch black inside with the curtains drawn and she tripped over piles of things that littered the floor. She heard soft snoring from the bed and muttered expletives under her breath as she made her way to the curtains.

"Rise and shine," she called loudly as she flung them open letting the watery pre-dawn light filter into the room.

"What the—" Cody hissed, bolting upright in his massive bed.

"Good morning to you too."

Cody rubbed his eyes like he couldn't believe them. "Hannah?"

"You overslept and now we're behind schedule. Grab your things and let's go."

"What time is it?" he grumbled.

"Time to go to school! We have a deal, remember? It starts today."

"I remember," he muttered.

Cody pulled the covers back revealing his toned body, his finer assets barely covered by his bright orange boxer briefs. They were the first splash of color in the house and Hannah's eyes shot straight for his healthy bulge.

Blush burnt her cheeks and she turned away so quickly she tripped over the pile of clothes on the floor and fell flat on her ass.

Cody's soft chuckling only made her cheeks hotter. He was standing over her offering his hand to help her up. She refused it and got to her feet herself. "Put some clothes on, please" she barked.

"Jesus, Hannah. I'm wearing underwear. Calm down."

"We're late," she steamed, ignoring his comments.

"Fine. Give me five minutes."

Cody disappeared into the adjoining bathroom suite and shut the door. She heard the toilet flush and then the shower turn on. She looked for somewhere to sit down, but just about every square inch of Cody's room was covered in clothes. *How could someone with so many maids have such a disastrous room?* Hannah decided the bed seemed the safest place to wait. She smoothed the comforter and perched on the edge. A minute later the shower squeaked off and Cody emerged from the bathroom, glistening with only a towel wrapped low around his waist. Hannah averted her eyes and stood up abruptly. *Mistake.* Cody must've been walking toward her when she looked down because she smacked straight into his wet chest. She gasped as his arms wrapped around her to steady her.

"Shit, did you chug a pot of coffee before you got here or something? Why are you so jumpy?"

"I'm not jumpy. I'm just not used to being accosted by half dressed men."

Cody snorted. "Wow, you've never seen a naked guy before, have you?"

"I don't see how that's any of your business," she shot back crossing her arms and taking a step back from him.

"You haven't! Hannah, this is the shit I'm talking about. You're never going to survive Harrison's ball if you react like this every time you see a half naked guy."

"There's going to be naked guys there?"

"Hannah, what do you think goes on at Harrison's parties?"

"I don't know . . . dancing?"

Another snort. "This isn't *Pretty in Pink*."

"What?"

"Let me guess, you've never seen *Pretty in Pink*?"

"No. But it's your job to teach me how to fit in. I'm sure if I just practice—"

"You can't practice having a life, Hannah."

That comment hurt more than she cared to admit. She squared her shoulders and walked to the door. "Get dressed, Cody. I'll be in the car. And hurry up, because we apparently have a lot of work to do."

CHAPTER

7

The drive to school was tense. Neither Hannah nor Cody spoke until they arrived at Stanton. Hannah pulled through the gate and passed the student parking lot.

"Where are we going?" Cody asked.

"Sports Annex."

Cody cocked an eyebrow at her.

"I have tennis practice."

"At 5:30 in the morning?"

"No, at 5:00 in the morning. You made me late. So to make up for it you're going to return my serves."

"This wasn't part of our deal."

"Our deal was you ride to and from school with me and tell me everything I need to know. Since all you've done this morning is flash me, insult me and make me late for practice, I think you're going to return my serves to make it up to me."

Cody let out an exacerbated sigh, but followed Hannah from the athletic lot to the tennis complex.

"Where is everyone?" he asked when he scanned the empty courts.

Hannah was already stretching. "What do you mean?"

"The rest of the tennis team?"

Hannah laughed. "You're looking at the tennis team."

"You come out here all by yourself to practice?"

"Yes."

"Where's your coach?"

"You don't know much about my tennis record, do you?"

Cody shrugged.

"I haven't been coached since I was twelve. I'm ranked number one in the state."

Cody smirked. "Of course you are."

"You don't believe me?" she asked, offended.

"No, I believe you. You're number one at everything you do, aren't you? Little Miss Perfect."

"I'm not perfect."

"No, I'm pretty sure you're perfect compared to me," Cody muttered.

"True. I don't have a DUI and I've never been to rehab," Hannah retorted while stretching out her hamstrings. She was busy pondering the other things she'd never done when she heard the metal door to the courts slam shut. She looked up just in time to see the back of Cody's green army jacket as he stalked to the parking lot.

Hannah was on her feet in no time, sprinting after him. She caught up to him quickly and grabbed his shoulder.

"Hey! Where are you going? We're not done."

"Oh we're done, Hannah. I'm not doing this. Take your stupid key and leave me alone," Cody yelled angrily pulling a skeleton key from his pocket and jamming it in

Hannah's hand.

"Why are you so angry?" Hannah asked in shock.

"Because. You just waltzed into my life yesterday and took over. You think you have me pegged? Some rich fuck up, right? Everyone else has exploited me, so why not you? I've got news for you, Hannah, you don't know me. And I don't owe you anything," Cody shouted before stalking away.

"Well you obviously don't know me either if you think for one second that I won't turn in your real test scores," Hannah shouted after him.

Cody halted. His back stiffened and he marched back to Hannah. "I didn't ask for your pity," he hissed. "You decided I wasn't worth your precious time and passed me all on your own."

"That's not why I did it. And besides, who do you think the administration will believe?"

"Why is this so fucking important to you?"

"Because you're right, okay? I've spent my whole life trying to be perfect and I'm terrified that it's cost me a life! I only have a few weeks left to make the high school memories that I thought weren't important! I'm sorry I had to blackmail you but I don't even have a single friend here. I don't know anyone who will help me," she whispered.

Cody scrubbed his large hands over his face and sighed. "Well that's the first real thing you've said to me, so we'll call it progress."

"So you'll help me?"

"Yes. But on three conditions. You have to be truthful with me, do what I say without question, and we work quickly. I have things I need to do, too."

"Deal!"

CHAPTER

8

Cody shook his head as he watched Hannah walk back to the courts, her tight little skirt hugging her ass as she marched ahead of him. *Shit.* This girl was going to be trouble and he didn't need anymore of that in his life.

He pretended not to watch Hannah stretch, but it was impossible. Her body was effortlessly fit, no doubt from years of tennis. Her long legs went on for miles, strong and nimble. She bent to touch her toes and Cody took a steadying breath. *Down boy. This one's not for you.* But no matter what he told himself, he couldn't deny his attraction to her. Hannah was hot. But there could never be anything between them. Good girls like Hannah Stark didn't date world-class losers like Cody. Plus even if he thought he had a chance in hell with her, she'd never take him seriously. The best he could hope for was to have a little fun. If he just played along he could get through this. Then he'd graduate and leave this place full of ghosts behind.

Done stretching, Hannah unlocked the utility room attached to the courts and grabbed a spare racket for Cody and a bucket of balls.

"Here," she said handing him the racket. "This one should do. Do you know how to play?"

"I've seen it on TV. Doesn't look too hard."

It was Hannah's time to arch an eyebrow. "I'll go easy on you. Just try and return my serves."

"Don't go easy. I play basketball. I think I can handle a little tennis ball."

"You *used* to play basketball," she reminded him.

"Lesson number one. Don't correct people when they're wrong."

"But—"

"Rule number two. Don't ask questions."

Hannah sighed. "So you're telling me that people like to be wrong?"

"No, people want to be right. But more importantly they don't want to be called out when they're wrong. Especially the Goldens."

Hannah nodded.

"Let's make this interesting," Cody smirked. "You serve and for every ball I return you answer a question."

"Why do—"

"Rule number two!"

Hannah sighed. "Don't ask questions."

"That's right. Besides. I need to get to know you to figure out what I'm dealing with. Unless you're afraid I'll tarnish your perfect record, tennis pro."

"You're on." A coy smile danced across Hannah's lips as she stretched her arm high and released a powerful serve at Cody's head.

"Shit!" Cody dove out of the way. "You know we're on the same team, right?"

Hannah laughed. "How about you get to ask a question even if you don't return my serve?"

"Just serve. I'll be ready this time."

"Suit yourself."

Hannah reached up again and slammed another ball Cody's way. He barely managed to dodge it and stay on his feet. She knew he was nowhere near returning any of her serves today. "At this rate you're not going to get to ask any questions."

"Fine. Why are you so good at tennis? Is it your passion?"

Hannah rolled her eyes. "No. My dad taught me to play when I was five. He said it would help my mental focus."

"And does it?"

"Yes. It's taught me precision, focus, boundaries, dedication, strategy, how to spot an opponent's weakness and deconstruct them. Like you, you're weak on your left," she said before slamming another serve to his left side.

"That doesn't sound like any fun at all."

"Isn't basketball the same?"

Cody laughed. "God no. I love basketball. It's like poetry and music, and when your teammates are all playing in sync, it's like magic."

"That's an unrealistic description. Basketball is a sport. Not poetry or music. And there's no such thing as magic."

Cody groaned. "How is it possible that you're good at everything except having a normal conversation?"

"My communication skills are more than adequate."

"That's what I mean. No one talks like that, Hannah. The Goldens sure as hell don't."

"Okay. Then teach me how they talk."

"One step at a time. I'm trying to find out where to start with you."

"Fine. Next question."

"Have you really never seen a naked guy before?"

"Why does that matter?"

"Rules one and two," Cody quipped narrowly missing the tennis ball he swung for.

Hannah rolled her eyes and sighed. "Fine. No I've never seen a naked guy. No guy has ever seen me naked. I've never had a boyfriend. I've never been kissed. I've never been on a date. Anything else embarrassing you'd like to know?"

"Hannah! How is that possible?"

"I don't know? You're the one who's supposed to have the answers."

"Are you straight?"

"Yes!"

"Are you sure?"

"I think so."

Cody sighed deeply and wiped his forehead. He marched up to the net and beckoned Hannah to join him by curling his finger at her. When she met him he reached across the net and pulled her to him, roughly locking his lips with hers. Hannah gasped into his mouth in surprise. Cody took that as an invitation to shove his tongue down her throat. She shoved him off and slapped him hard.

"What the hell was that?" she yelled.

He smiled, rubbing his cheek. "Just checking."

"For what, cavities?"

"To see if you're straight."

Her eyes widened. "And?" she demanded, hands on her hips.

"I mean you're difficult to talk to, super conceded, but you're not hopeless. Now you can even say you've had your first kiss."

Hannah scowled at Cody.

"Relax. You're pretty and that usually excuses all kinds of flaws."

"Flaws? And I am *not* hard to talk to."

"Hannah, if you want help you have to be open to the truth and that might mean criticism."

"I can agree to that. But we need a strategy. It just feels like you're picking on me."

"You mean like I'm sizing up my opponent to spot their weaknesses?" he said mockingly.

Hannah frowned.

"Relax. Unlike you, I'm looking for your weaknesses so I can help you fix them."

"That *is* the deal."

"So, let's study the evidence, brainiac. You've never had a boyfriend. Never been on a date. You had to blackmail me to get a party invite. And you only just had your first kiss."

"How . . . how was it?"

"What, the kiss?" Cody asked not trying to conceal his smile.

Hannah felt her cheeks flush, but she needed to know. She shoved down her embarrassment and nodded.

"Well I can tell it was your first kiss," he smirked.

"Is that bad?"

Cody winked. "Nah. Nothing a little practice won't fix."

"Practice." Hannah repeated the word slowly. Practice was something she could do. Something she was good at. Hell, she was the poster child for practice makes perfect.

"And you'll help me practice kissing?"

He feigned frustration. "If I must."

"So you'll be like my practice boyfriend?"

Cody rolled his eyes. "Why do girls insist on labeling things?"

Hannah cocked her head in confusion. "Labels help clarify things. It's something both men and women use equally. I believe women to be the superior of our species, so perhaps that's why you assume women use labels more often?"

"It was a joke, Hannah. But why don't you get your sweet cheeks back on the court, tennis pro, and I'll show you the superior species."

Hannah blinked while Cody retreated to his corner of the court—ball and racket in hand.

"By the way, *that's* how normal high school students speak," Cody added with a smirk. He bounced the ball, getting ready to serve.

"Bring it on," Hannah called.

"That's it. You almost sound human."

If it was practice Cody wanted, that's what he'd get. Hannah was prepared to kick his butt on the tennis court and then kiss him all night! Nothing was going to get in the way of her plan.

She took a swig of her water bottle and spun her tennis racket waiting for Cody to serve. He sent the ball sailing far over her head. She laughed out loud when it flew over the fence.

"That was my practice shot," Cody called.

"There's no do over's in life, Cody."

"You've got that right," he muttered picking up another ball and lobbing it across the net.

Hannah smiled. This was too easy. She put some back-spin on it and fired directly at Cody. He dove out of the way and she couldn't suppress her laughter.

"You still want to serve?" she taunted.

"Ok champ. You proved your point. You own the tennis court. But we'll see how good you are when you're on my courts."

"I don't play basketball. I'm sure I'll be awful."

"I thought you were good at everything."

"I'm confident I can master anything with the right amount of practice."

Cody rolled his eyes and Hannah glanced at her watch.

"Last question. I've got to shower before class."

"Alright. Why is going to Harrison's party so important to you?" Cody asked as Hannah slammed a ball in his direction.

"Because I want Harrison and the rest of our class to *see* me. I want to be Hannah, the girl, for once. Not Hannah, the genius that no one talks to unless they need help with homework. I want to do something wild and carefree. I want to make memories."

"Where is this sudden urge coming from?"

"You sound like a psychologist," Hannah said wrinkling her nose as she squinted into the harsh morning sunlight.

"My shrink would be so proud."

"You see a psychologist?" she asked, sounding surprised.

"You kill your girlfriend and try not needing a shrink." Cody's jovial mood vanished. "I think that's enough for now."

CHAPTER
9

Cody walked back to the main campus alone. Hannah promised to shower quickly, but he didn't want to wait. He wanted to get as far away from her as possible before he lost it. As always, at the slightest mention of Elena's death, his self-loathing kicked in. He'd been battling this crippling depression for a year but nothing seemed to lighten the lead weight he carried in his heart.

Strangely, sparring with Hannah allowed him to forget his pain momentarily. But when she'd headed to the locker room to shower, Cody was left alone with his thoughts and the pain came rushing back tenfold. It was almost crueler—chastising him for forgetting his sins for even the briefest of moments.

Distance and solitude were the only things that helped. Something Cody worried would become harder to find with Hannah in his life.

Hannah spotted Cody on the quad and ran over, waving her cell phone to get his attention. "Did you get my message?" she asked.

"Ya mean the relationships for dummies list? Yeah, I got it," Cody frowned staring at the bullet point list Hannah sent to his phone.

"It's the list of practice boyfriend tasks. Do you have any others to add?"

"Uh, no."

"Haven't you been working on a strategy?"

"No, I was actually in class for the past few hours."

"Doing what?"

"Doing class work, Hannah! We're not all geniuses."

"You said you wanted to work quickly. I assumed you meant you'd be focused on this."

Cody rolled his eyes. "I am. All we need to do is get you noticed. Start a buzz, that kind of thing."

"Okay, how do we do that?"

Cody glanced around the campus. His eyes landed on the Golden Gate. It was full of Goldens enjoying their lunches and gossiping. "Come with me."

"Where are we going?" Hannah protested as Cody dragged her by the arm toward the bridge. He squeezed harder and she yelped his name!

"Cody! Stop!"

That's it. Just a little bit further. He glanced up and smiled, noting he'd gained the attention of more than a few Goldens. Hannah was a natural and she didn't even know it.

Cody tugged harder knowing how Hannah would react.

"I said stop!" she yelled digging her heels into the ground.

Cody stopped pulling her and she nearly fell backward. He took the opportunity to catch her while she was off balance. He wrapped his arms around her and locked his lips with hers ferociously. She gasped and went limp for a moment before coming to her senses and playing right into his hand. She walloped him with a slap that made him see stars. Cody suddenly knew why she was so good at tennis. *Hannah had an arm on her!*

"What *the* hell was that?" she screeched.

Cody shrugged and smirked. "Just a bit of fun," he whispered.

Hannah was fuming. She took off back toward the school and Cody yelled after her. "Ah, come on, doll face. Don't be mad at me. You know I can't help it."

Hannah didn't look back, but Cody did. His plan had worked flawlessly. The Golden Gate was full of slack jawed students.

CHAPTER

10

It was after school by the time Cody found Hannah again. She was waiting for him in her car looking none too pleased when he swung his lanky body into the passenger seat.

"Hey, doll face," he greeted her.

"That wasn't funny, Cody. We're practicing to prove a point, not just so you can get off whenever you want."

"Ya know, you're pretty good at slinging insults for someone who isn't good at *talking*. And for your information, I wasn't *getting off*. I was getting you the attention you need. The whole Golden Gate saw us kiss and then you slap me. That instantly gives you points in their eyes."

"Really?"

"Really. The Goldens hate me after . . . well everything that happened last year."

"So because I slapped you, they'll like me?"

"It's a step in the right direction. They'll definitely want to talk to you to get the gossip."

"So what do we do now?" she asked pulling out of the school lot.

"Take a right."

"But home is—"

"Hannah! What's rule number two?"

"Fine. But I'll be a better driver if I know where we're going."

"Shopping. You need to dress the part."

"What's wrong with how I dress?"

"Nothing, if you're running for congress."

❦

To Hannah's dismay, Cody was directing her to the luxury district in the heart of Boston, not the outlet mall she was used to doing her shopping at. She cringed when she pulled up to Neiman Marcus and the valet opened the creaking door to her rust-bitten Volvo. It didn't fit in with BMW's, Audi's and Mercedes that lined the glowing glass-fronts of the posh street.

"I don't have any cash," Hannah hissed when Cody came around to her side.

He winked at the valet and simply muttered, "Matthews," before taking her hand and leading her into the gigantic department store. "You don't pay the valet here. It goes on your account."

"Oh," Hannah murmured, suddenly feeling like she didn't have a clue how the Goldens lived.

A petite brunette clerk rushed up to Cody the moment they were inside the glittering department store. "Mr. Matthews! We've missed you. And who is this?" The woman's perfectly sculpted eyebrow arched as she took in Hannah.

"Hello, Bianca. This is my girlfriend, Hannah Stark."

"Girlfriend!" Bianca barely recovered her composure. "Good for you," she added softly touching Cody's arm. "It's about time you start dating again." Then she turned her attention to Hannah. "Miss Stark, it's a pleasure," Bianca purred.

Hannah smiled politely and shook Bianca's perfectly manicured hand, sensing she wasn't pleased in the least to be touching Hannah. She really couldn't blame the delicate sales woman. She looked like she'd been meticulously steamed and pressed. There wasn't a crease anywhere on her, including her plastic-like complexion.

"What can I assist you with? Are we shopping for anything in particular today?" Bianca asked as she eyeballed Hannah with distain, probably wondering where to start.

From her scuffed loafers to her clearance rack cardigan, Hannah felt like a street urchin compared to the patrons in Neiman Marcus. Even the mannequins seemed to be looking down at her.

Luckily Cody saved her. "We'll be doing our shopping on our own today," he replied graciously and tucked Hannah's hand under her arm, pulling her away from Bianca's judgy little eyes.

"Do you not usually do your own shopping?" Hannah asked when they were out of earshot.

Cody snorted. "Bianca's my family's personal shopper. I come in once a year to have my measurements taken and then she just sends things to the house for me."

"Seriously? That's ridiculous."

He shrugged. "You're the one who wants to be a Golden. This is how it's done."

Hannah noticed that Cody didn't say it was how *he* did things. *Did he really not consider himself a Golden?* Maybe the kids at school had kicked him out of their little elitist club, but it seemed the rest of the upper crust was still happy to take his money. She sighed deeply. *Perhaps she'd underestimated how difficult it would be to crack the Goldens.*

"Is this really necessary," Hannah groaned as Cody navigated the racks of mesmerizing apparel with ease.

"Not much of a shopper, are ya?"

Hannah frowned. She wasn't opposed to shopping. It was the blinding price tags that were making her sweat.

As if sensing her distress, Cody laughed. "Come on, I have a feeling we're gonna need a pick-me-up if we're gonna get through this."

"Starbucks?"

"What did you think I meant?"

Remembering one of Cody's earlier lessons, Hannah kept her comments to herself. He probably didn't want to hear that she'd assumed he meant drugs or something illegal when he mentioned a pick-me-up.

They stood in line listening to obnoxious coffee orders being slung at the barista like some foreign language.

"What would you like?" Cody asked as they approached the counter.

Hannah stared at the board in wonder. *What language was this?* Some of the words were in Italian, some English and frankly some just seemed made up.

"Um, I don't know. I don't drink coffee." Hannah admitted sheepishly.

"What? Hannah, are you Mormon or something? Because I draw the line at destroying your religious faith."

"No. I'm not Mormon. But it's good to know you have some morals."

"Are you sure? No coffee, no sex, no fun. . ."

Hanna rolled her eyes and elbowed Cody in the side, which only made him laugh.

"How does Miss Perfect stay up late and study without coffee?"

Hannah scoffed at his dig. "I don't need coffee. It's a drug you know?"

Cody smirked. "Well it's one drug you're gonna have to get used to if you want to mingle with the Goldens outside of school. Spotting them without their Starbucks and cell phones glued to their hands is like spotting Bigfoot."

"Fine. Can you just order me something mild?"

Cody laughed. "And here I thought you wanted to be wild."

When it was their turn to order, he asked for two vanilla lattes. The barista looked grateful for the simple order and quickly served them. They retreated to a high-top in the corner of the coffee shop and sipped their lattes.

"So what'd ya think?" Cody asked gesturing to the coffee mug.

"It's delicious. I can see how people get addicted to these."

"I knew you'd be a latte girl."

"Is that a good thing, or are you making fun of me again?"

"It's not really a thing. It's just you. You're *so* vanilla latte."

"You mean mild and boring."

"You said it."

"You're right. I *am* boring. But that's why I have to do this. I have the rest of my life to be boring vanilla-latte-Hannah. Harrison's party is my only chance to be wild-and-free-Hannah."

"What, Brown's not known for its wild party scene?"

"How do you know I'm going to Brown?"

"Everyone knows you're going to Brown, Hannah. The school posted it on the bulletin board freshman year," Cody teased. "It's been up there so long it's turning yellow."

"Oh."

"Don't worry, you'll have your wild and crazy night. We just need to get you some new clothes, create some more buzz about you dating a bad boy and you'll be *Golden*."

"Ha ha, very funny."

"Look at you! Already picking up on my sarcasm. Perhaps there's hope for you yet." Cody grinned and stood up. "Come on let's take these to go."

He led Hannah to the counter to get to go cups when a swirl of pink cashmere and glossy blonde hair cut them off—Savannah Huxley.

"I ordered an iced, half caff, ristretto, venti, four-pumps, sugar-free, cinnamon-dolce, soy, skinny, latte, no whip. This is clearly not sugar-free!"

"Was that even English?" Hannah whispered to Cody, who laughed.

Hearing their laughter, Savannah whirled around about to direct her wrath at them. But her mouth hung open when her eyes took in Cody, and then Hannah.

"Oh my god, Cody and . . . Hannah, right?"

44

Hannah nodded.

"I didn't know you two were an item."

"That's because you weren't supposed to," Cody replied taking Hannah's hand and dragging her quickly from the coffee shop.

"What did you do that for?" Hannah howled when they'd escaped Savannah's glare. "That was my chance to talk to her."

"Lesson number two. Always leave them wanting more."

CHAPTER

11

Hannah's day had gotten stranger after the coffee shop. She somehow stepped into a strange subculture that she didn't know existed. One where torture was disguised as pampering, shopping the sales was taboo and being spotted with an empty glass of champagne in hand turned clerks into track stars, racing to fill your glass.

Cody had been able to politely decline—with his reputation and all—but Hannah gave in after Cody's taunts about being wild and free.

At least she could check underage drinking off her list, she thought while sipping the delightful bubbles. She was convinced it was the only reason she survived her first—and hopefully last—eyebrow wax. The mani-pedi was almost enjoyable, but Hannah ran from the spa when they explained what a Brazilian wax was.

She currently sat motionless at the makeup counter while two artists perfected her *flaws*. Hannah found it funny that she'd never noticed her *flaws* before, but after Roderick and Hector pointed them out and quickly caked the right makeup or lotion over them, she wondered how she'd ever survived without them.

"Voila! You're perfection, darling!" Roderick exclaimed after an hour of primping.

Hannah was stunned when she saw her refection. She looked just like Bianca—polished and plastic. "Thank you," she said in awe raising her hand to touch her flawless skin.

Hector slapped her hand away. "No touching!"

"You like?" Roderick asked Cody, who was busy texting. He looked up for a moment. "Yes, very much."

"What account will we be putting the products on today?" Hector asked.

"Matthews," Cody replied.

"Splendid."

Roderick handed Hannah a gigantic shopping bag full of cosmetics, creams, spritzes and strange looking applicators. *How was she ever going to replicate their masterpiece on her own?* She kept her concern to herself and thanked them, letting Cody lead her away.

"Come on, doll face, your new wardrobe awaits," he declared steering her through the brightly lit aisles to a doorway labeled 'fitting rooms'.

"Must you call me doll face?"

"Do you prefer Miss Perfect? Or maybe sweet cakes, snookums—"

Hannah huffed. "Never mind. Doll face is fine!"

"Great, then on to the fitting rooms, doll face."

Cody's grin was infectious but Hannah was exhausted. It was already 7 pm. She was normally in bed by 8 or 9 at the latest and she still hadn't eaten dinner.

"Do we have to?" she groaned.

"Yes! How are you *not* loving this? It's your Pretty Woman moment. I thought that was every girl's fantasy?"

"I was already a pretty woman, thank you very much!"

"No! Pretty Woman . . . the movie."

Hannah stared at him blankly.

"Julia Roberts and Richard Gere?"

She just blinked in confusion.

"You're kidding me! You've never seen Pretty Woman?"

"I'm not really into movies. Unless it's a historical documentary. They fascinate me."

Cody shook his head in amazement.

"What?"

"You're the strangest girl I've ever met."

"So all girls like this Pretty Woman movie?" Hannah asked.

"Yeah, it's about a prostitute that gets hired by a lonely rich guy who buys her all these expensive things and they fall in love."

"So the rich guy has to buy the love of the prostitute? That sounds terrible!"

Cody laughed. "Well when you say it that way . . . you just have to see it. I'm adding movie night to your research. Starting with Pretty Woman. And then there's some teen movies you should watch to learn how to talk like a normal human. It'll help you spot when guys are being creeps and girls are being fake too."

Hannah's face lit up. "That's a brilliant idea." She pulled her phone from her purse and opened her notes app, ready to write down movie titles. "Pretty Woman. What else?"

"Calm down, Spielberg. Just come over this weekend and we'll have a Netflix marathon, cause you're gonna need my commentary."

She nodded and slipped the phone back into her purse.

"Now get in there an try on some clothes," Cody commanded, nodding to the row of white doors.

"But we didn't pick any out yet?"

"What'd you think I was doing the whole time you were getting pampered?"

"Playing on your phone?"

"I was texting Bianca. She filled the fitting room with everything you'll need."

"What happened to doing our own shopping?"

"I didn't want to hurt her feelings," he said with an apologetic smirk. "Now quit stalling and try on your clothes. And you better show me everything. I'm not letting any boring khakis or frumpy sweaters slip by."

"Cody, it's not that I don't appreciate all of this Pretty Woman pampering." Hannah lowered her voice to a whisper. "But I can't afford to buy my clothes here."

"It's on me."

"But—"

"Lesson number three. Never decline your boyfriend's gifts. Besides, you're helping me."

"How?"

"My dad feels less guilty for never being around when he buys me things. He'll sleep easier when he sees his Neiman Marcus bill this month. Now no more arguing. Get in there." He slapped Hannah's ass and she yelped, but made her way into the fitting room.

The entire room was white—walls, doors, mirrors,

floors. It was blinding. It was the largest fitting room Hannah had ever seen. A white wing-backed chair with an ottoman judged her from the corner. Next to it was a silver doorbell labeled 'assistance'. Hannah glanced at the long rack filled with the clothes Bianca had picked out. *This was going to take all night!*

Hannah suddenly felt the need to sit down. Luckily a huge white tufted-bench with silver legs had been provided. It was over six feet long! *How many people were they expecting in the fitting room at once?*

Hannah looked up and shook her head at the ornate chandelier sparkling above her. She was so out of her league.

She took a deep breath and fanned through the clothing, settling on what she was most comfortable with first—a pair of dark jeans, white linen shirt and a camel-colored blazer. The skinny jeans were skintight and bending her knees was a struggle, but the rich fabric of the buttery blazer and the finely tailored shirt made up for her discomfort. Hannah gazed at her reflection in awe. She looked like a million bucks. In one afternoon she'd gone from high school nerd to the beautiful, confident career woman she longed to be.

She slid her feet into a gorgeous pair of herringbone Tory Burch flats and had to restrain herself from skipping back to the posh white waiting area, where Cody was waiting. When he gazed up from his phone he frowned. *Not what Hannah was expecting.*

"Ugh." Cody gave a thumbs down.

"What's wrong with this?"

"The clothes are perfect, it's the way you're wearing them."

Cody was on his feet, pulling the hem of Hannah's blouse from her jeans and unbuttoning it to her breastbone.

When his hand grazed her chest, she slapped him.

"Don't get me wrong, I like the whole feisty thing, but it might sell the whole boyfriend thing better if you could refrain from slapping me every time I touch you," he whispered.

"I'm sorry. It's just my instinct. I'm not used to having people touch me. I'm not sure I see the appeal."

"Seriously?"

"I don't know. I've never had a boyfriend, remember? I just need to practice more."

Cody sighed and dragged Hannah back to the fitting room.

"What are you doing?"

"Practicing."

CHAPTER

12

"You're not supposed to be in here."

"Says who?" Cody asked, looking around the massive white room and locking the door behind him.

They were completely alone. Hannah gazed at the 'assistance' button and fought her urge to push it repeatedly as Cody moved closer to her. He popped the collar of her shirt and blazer, tying a blue and gold Chanel scarf around her throat. He ran his hands down her body, unbuttoning the untucked bottom of her blouse.

Hannah's pulse pounded in her ears as Cody's hands continued their path down her legs. He slipped off her flats and held a pair of classic red pumps up. She slipped her feet in and he stood up to examine her.

He scratched his chin. "Better," he said placing his hands on her hips to spin her toward the mirror. "And you haven't slapped me once."

Hannah was grateful for the makeup staining her cheeks.

It helped hide the massive blush heating her body from Cody's touch. *He was right. She needed a lot more practice. And she could suddenly see the appeal of having his hands all over her.*

"Memorize this outfit. You're wearing it to school to-morrow."

"I can't. We have uniforms."

"Wear your skirt instead of jeans, and your vest under the blazer."

Hannah swallowed and nodded, nervous at the thought of not following the Stanton dress code to the letter. But Cody was right. That's how the Goldens dressed—mixing and matching parts of their uniforms with posh statement pieces that probably cost a fortune.

"Next," he said handing her a dress before lounging in the wing-backed chair.

"You want me to change in front of you?"

Cody sighed deeply. "Hannah, you're the one who wanted to practice. You need to be comfortable with yourself and your body. If you can't get undressed in front of your *boyfriend* how are you going to be able to handle yourself at Harrison's party?"

"Right. I forgot about that bit," she said biting her lip nervously. "Are you sure there's going to be naked people there?"

"There's always naked people at his parties."

"Oh . . ."

"Lesson number four. Any good high school party is about three things. Getting drunk, getting naked or getting high."

❧

Cody took one look at Hannah's petrified doe eyes and almost called the whole stupid thing off. The poor girl had no idea what she was getting herself into. Harrison and the rest of the Goldens would eat her alive. *And for what? To prove a point?* Hannah didn't need to prove anything to anyone. Especially the Goldens. She was too good for them anyway. *Too good for me too,* Cody reminded himself. But before he could say anything she was undressing.

His throat dried up completely as he watched her shrug off the thin white shirt.

Shit! She was hot. He'd gotten a glimpse that morning, but that body! *Tennis was good to her.* Cody was having trouble remembering why he was still sitting in the chair instead of tearing her bra off. That was until Hannah tried to peel off her skinny jeans and fell over, nearly taking the whole rack of clothes with her.

Cody rushed to help her. "You okay?"

"Sure. What's a little more embarrassment for today?"

He laughed. "Don't worry. I'm pretty sure it's impossible to look sexy while taking off skinny jeans."

"Let's make that a rule. Don't take skinny jeans off in front of others."

"How about this? Rule number five. Let your boyfriend take off your jeans," he winked tugging her feet free from the stretchy denim that was strangling her ankles. Taking her hands he pulled her to her feet.

"Thanks," she smiled and then seemed to realize she was standing in front of him in nothing but her bra and underwear. She squealed and grabbed a dress from the rack, trying to cover herself up."

"Hannah, stop. You have nothing to be embarrassed

about. You're beautiful," Cody said softly, finding he meant every word. She was stunning, smart, sexy, funny . . . He was suddenly having a hard time keeping his hands off of her. He didn't want to be practice.

Get your head out of the gutter, Cody mentally scolded himself. *She is way out of your league.*

He mentally checked himself and took a step forward, and tugged the dress, but Hannah held tight.

"Hannah, you don't need to cover up who you are. Lesson number six. If you can face your fears in your underwear you can conquer the world."

She scoffed. "Easy for someone completely clothed to say."

Cody arched an eyebrow and shrugged off his green army jacket. He peeled off his black v-neck t-shirt and kicked off his shoes. He was starting to unbuckle his belt when Hannah loosed a breath loudly.

"Fine! You proved you're not shy . . . you're conquering the world or whatever!"

"Your turn," Cody ordered.

Hannah balked, fear chilling her flushed skin. Cody moved toward her, slowly tugging the dress from her hands. She stood before him in her white bra and panties. They were plain as could be, but he didn't give a shit. All he could think about was the perfection that was hiding beneath them. Hannah was visibly shaking as Cody took another step closer, pressing his chest into hers. Hannah's breath caught in her throat, her bright blue eyes widening.

Practice! Hannah reminded herself. *Don't freak out. This is just practice.*

But she couldn't help it. She *was* freaking out. Her body refused to listen to her mind. All she could see was the gold flecks in Cody's light brown eyes smoldering through his dark lashes. Her heart pounded against his chest, her body shaking as she watched his delicious lips move toward hers. She closed her eyes, willing herself not to be so nervous.

Hannah nearly jumped out of her skin when Cody's breath tickled her ear—hot and close. "Hannah, I promise I won't ever hurt you."

She trembled.

"Look at me."

Her eyes flew open and she stared at his handsome face. Something changed. He didn't look smug or sarcastic. He looked . . . kind . . . sincere. He was a different person all together. One that she was suddenly drawn toward.

Cody's voice was firm. "You're in charge here, okay?"

She nodded.

"Tell me what you want."

Hannah's breath caught in her throat when he pulled her closer, running his hands seductively down her sides. Her body came alive in a way she'd never experienced before, pulsing with heat and desire as her chest pushed against Cody's. She stiffened and melted all at once under his touch. She couldn't believe she was standing in such close proximity to him in nothing but her underwear. *And she didn't hate it.* That thought alone terrified her.

"Hannah, tell me what you want me to do."

She nodded.

He smirked. "That means use your words."

There was the mockery she was used to.

She rolled her eyes. "I don't know what I want. That's the problem. I'm no good at this."

"You're doing fine. You're just wound up. You need to chill. What do you do in a tennis match when you need to stay calm?"

She shook her head.

"Tell me."

"No. You're going to make fun of me."

"I promise I won't."

She sighed. "I breathe and make mental lists."

Cody cocked an eyebrow.

"Don't judge, it works."

"Okay, give it a whirl," he said pulling her closer to him.

Her breath hitched instantly when he pressed his body into hers.

"Breathe," Cody reminded her.

She closed her eyes and took a deep steadying breath and mentally repeated her mantra.

Keep your eye on the prize, Hannah.

Get the key.

Get the guy.

Make memories.

High school perfection.

When she opened her eyes, Cody's handsome face filled her vision. *God, he was gorgeous.* Hannah began to second-guess her decision to choose such an attractive boy to practice these things with. Being this close to Cody made it impossible to focus. She had to close her eyes and start her list all over again. This time she reminded herself of who he was, training her mind to see the boy with no future who owed her.

This time when she opened her eyes, her head remained clear and she knew exactly what she wanted—perfection. She would settle for nothing less.

⁓

When Hannah opened her eyes she looked different, confident. Her technique had worked.

"What do you want to practice, Hannah. The ball's in your court."

She looked up at him assertively. "This," she whispered, wrapping her arms around his neck and kissing him.

It only took Cody a second to respond. His arms circled her slender waist and he kissed her back with passion. Hannah parted her lips, teasing his tongue with hers. Cody eagerly answered by pressing her harder against him, nearly pulling her off her feet.

She stood on her tiptoes and wound her fingers through his thick dark hair. He groaned into her mouth and her body responded. Her heat rushed to him, her heart hammering against Cody's erratically. His hands gripped her tightly. She was like a ball of rubber bands, he could feel each touch winding tighter and tighter.

Hannah leaned into Cody as his hands roamed down to her hips. She moved her trembling fingers down his bare chest and timidly hooked them into the waist of his jeans. But as soon as she touched his scorching skin, his muscles tensed and he pulled away, breaking the frantic spell they'd been under.

Cody's eyes were wide as he watched Hannah nervously touch her lips.

"Was that good?" she asked.

"That's enough for today," Cody said grabbing his clothes. "Get dressed. I'll meet you in the car," he grumbled before storming from the fitting room.

He left Hannah gaping at him in shock. The sound of the slamming door barely audible above the turmoil screaming beneath his veins.

CHAPTER
13

Hannah lay on her bed wondering what the hell she'd done wrong? The ride home with Cody had been awkward and silent. After he fled from the fitting room like he discovered she had smallpox, she stumbled around trying to find her clothes amongst the expensive apparel littering the floor. It didn't seem right to leave the gorgeous fabrics lying around so Hannah did her best to hang them back up.

A million thoughts had raced through her mind as she tidied up the fitting room. The most prevalent one was that kissing her was probably some sort of cruel and unusual form of punishment for Cody. He was used to beautiful, well-practiced girls. Maybe asking him to be her practice boyfriend wasn't fair. He owed her, but she was starting to feel like she was taking things too far. With how fast he'd bolted she was worried she was causing him to be physically ill.

The odd thing was, before he'd run out, she had felt something. Kissing him didn't seem like practice at all. It felt

. . . right. More than right, it was amazing. Hannah had never experienced such a rush of nervous excitement before.

She touched her lips at the memory of their kiss and sighed. She was being stupid. She couldn't possibly have felt anything for Cody. That's why she'd picked him. He was safe. She'd never fall for someone as screwed up as he was. And she was certain he didn't feel anything for her. He'd barely said two words the whole car ride home. He was already up the stairs to his massive house when she shouted, "pick you up tomorrow."

His only response was a wave. He didn't even bother to look back at her.

"Ugh! What a jerk!"

Hannah sat up and punched her pillow, frustrated that her plan was falling apart because Cody was being a flake. All he'd done was force feed her caffeine, subject her to torturous primping, make her take her clothes off, tell her she needed new ones and then left without letting her get any. She reminded herself she didn't pick him for his charm. She was just going to have to suck it up and try harder. She wasn't going to let Cody Matthews stand in the way of her perfect high school résumé.

Dressed in her favorite oversized gray sweatshirt from Brown and plaid pajama bottoms, Hannah hunched in front of her computer screen. She was studying graduation speeches again when she heard the doorbell ring. She didn't flinch. She knew her father would answer. He was a night owl. Running his own tech company allowed him to work from home, but that meant he pretty much worked 24/7.

Hannah glanced at the clock. *Odd. Who would be stopping by so late?* It was 10 pm. *Way past her bedtime!* But she was too restless to sleep. *Stupid vanilla latte!*

The knock at her door startled her.

"Hannah?" Her father's voice called softly in the hallway. "Are you awake?"

She strode to the door and creaked it open. "I'm up. What's going on, Dad?"

"A currier just delivered a bunch of bags for you," he said holding up six gigantic silver bags. Each one with the words, Neiman Marcus, printed on the side. "There's more downstairs."

"Oh!" Hannah's heart skipped as she grabbed the bags from her father.

Cody came through!

"Thanks." Hannah quickly stashed the bags in her room and ran down to the foyer with her father trailing behind her. She spotted three more Neiman Marcus bags, half a dozen garment bags and a short, wide white bag with the words LA PERLA stamped on the side in bold silver letters. There was an envelope attached to the handle with her name on it.

"What is all of this for?" her father asked.

"School project," she snapped, scooping up the bags and running back up to her bedroom.

Hannah locked the door and breathlessly looked at the sea of department store bags covering her floor. *Where to start?* She went to the LA PERLA bag first since she was most curious about the note. Maybe Cody was apologizing for running out on her. *Maybe he really was sick. Oh god, maybe it was too hard for him to be around all the champagne. There was a bottle on ice in her fitting room. She'd been drinking it. Did she taste like champagne when she kissed him?*

She fumbled with the envelope praying she hadn't inadvertently sent him back to rehab.

'To conquer the world.' - C

Hannah flipped the card over and peered into the empty envelope, but that was it. There was nothing else. She unwrapped the white tissue paper inside and pulled out an extremely lacey, extremely see-through, sexy black bra. Hannah's cheeks burned scarlet when she pulled out the matching panties—thongs of course. The bag was full of six more identical sets in white, pale blue, soft pink, nude, red and gray.

"Holy hell!" Hannah exclaimed when she caught the price tag on the skimpy panties. She scanned the rest of the lingerie and did a quick calculation. She gasped out loud. There was over $5000 in underwear sprawled out on her bed!

"This is insane," she whispered.

She pawed through the rest of the bags, pulling out the lavish items and carefully laying them on her bed. Cody purchased every item from the fitting room! It was a small fortune. It would cover her entire tuition to Brown—not that she was paying to go there. She'd never be able to afford Brown if she hadn't gotten a full scholarship. But that wasn't the point. It was the principle. It made no sense to Hannah to spend that kind of money on clothes! No wonder it was impossible to reach Golden status at Stanton. If it required shopping habits like this there was no way Hannah would ever earn a way in on her own.

As dedicated as she was to her cause, Hannah was starting to feel uncomfortable with her and Cody's arrangement. At this rate, she was going to be the one who owed him.

"Not going to happen," she muttered grabbing her phone. She tapped out a quick text to Cody and hit send.

GOT THE BAGS. WAY TOO MUCH. I'M SEND-ING THEM BACK. – HANNAH

A bubble appeared on her screen. Cody was texting back.

RULE #2. LESSON #3. – CODY

"He can shove his ridiculous rules," Hannah muttered hitting the call button.

Cody answered on the first ring. "Hello, doll face."

"Cody, they're going back. All that stuff cost way too much money. I'm not comfortable with it."

"So you're okay with blackmail, but you draw the line at expensive apparel?" he mocked.

"It's absurd to spend that much money on clothes! And I can by my own underwear, thank you very much."

"Oh give it a rest, Hannah. You go to Stanton for Christ sake. You obviously have the means, so stop pretending to be offended by wealth. I'm over the whole innocent bit. And everyone knows you can't return lingerie, so deal with it."

Hannah was speechless.

"Hell-o?" Cody taunted when she didn't reply. "You still there?"

"Yeah," was all she could manage.

"Good. Then I expect to see you dressed accordingly tomorrow morning and put your game face on so we can get this over as quickly as possible."

Click.

Hannah sat in stunned silence after Cody hung up on her. She wasn't used to being caught off guard. *But what had she expected?* No one knew she attended Stanton Prep for free. Her father could never afford the steep tuition, but he wanted the best for her and always led by example. She still remembered the day he'd told her that he'd enrolled her in Stanton. "If you want something, you *make* it happen," he'd said.

When she attended her interview with the dean she'd found out the only way she'd been allowed to attend Stanton was because her father donated his company's software for the entire campus so she could attend for free. She felt horrible, knowing that he was giving away his hard work for free. Plus, it made her feel like an intruder. Even as a sixth grader, she knew that if her pauper status got around at Stanton she'd never fit in. So she kept to herself, focused on academics and made sure no one ever learned her secret.

Hearing Cody say she had money should have eased her nerves. It was further proof that she'd successfully managed to survive Stanton without anyone knowing she couldn't afford to be there. *So why was it bothering her so much?* It wasn't so much Cody's statement, but the way he'd said it. Implying that because she had money that she didn't need to value it. She hated the venomous entitlement in his voice.

Hannah squared her shoulders and walked to her closet to make room for her new wardrobe. *What's done was done,* she thought. If Cody was going to be pigheaded and arrogant she wasn't going to let the clothes go to waste. She'd call it an investment in her future. *And* a reminder to not turn into a Golden in her quest to conquer them.

She folded Cody's note and put it in her desk drawer, before hopping into bed.

"To conquer the world, indeed," she grumbled switching off the light.

CHAPTER

14

Cody felt bad after he hung up on Hannah. But just hearing her voice on the phone was enough to make him lose his resolve to continue their charade. After the fitting room incident he'd decided he was done. Graduating wasn't worth the emotional turmoil he'd gone through today. He'd nearly had a panic attack on the car ride home. He was barely holding it together as it was. The last thing he needed was some girl messing with his head and sending him straight back to rehab. All that would do was make certain he didn't graduate with his classmates.

But did he even care? The kids he'd known since grammar school, and considered his friends, dropped him like a bad habit the second being his friend became inconvenient to their social status. *So screw them. He didn't need them. He didn't need anyone.*

Maybe he could just get his GED. But he dismissed the thought instantly, knowing it would kill his father. He wasn't around much, but he'd sacrificed a lot to make sure Cody had every opportunity—including his marriage. Cody wasn't quite sure what happened between his parents. He was so young when they divorced. But it was clear that Cody was an unpleasant reminder of their failure. He couldn't let them down by adding more failure. He'd already done enough damage. It was time for him to grow up.

Cody had been more than happy to go through the motions for the next few weeks so he could put his high school nightmare to rest once and for all and move on. That was until Hannah screwed everything up.

How hard could it be, Cody? Give the girl your key, dress her up, introduce her to the douche bags that will be at the party and you're free. All you have to do is pretend to care about helping her for a few days.

"Pretend!" he scolded himself.

He didn't think it would be hard. Sure she was hot, but so was every girl at his school. But none of them were, Elena. None of them knew him or gave a shit about him. No one could fix what she had broken.

Elena's death had destroyed him and after rehab Cody vowed he would never let anyone in again. And it was working just fine until fucking Hannah Stark, with her big doe eyes and perky innocent breasts offered herself to him on a silver platter. *He didn't need this shit. Hadn't he been through enough?*

By the time he'd gotten out of Hannah's car Cody had convinced himself that he didn't care if she got her perfect high school experience or if he didn't graduate. But then he checked his phone. *Mistake.* The socialsphere was a twitter with talk about Cody and Hannah.

Spotted at school.

Spotted at Starbucks.

Definitely sleeping together.

Did you hear he got her pregnant too?

How long before he kills her?

OMG she deserves to die. Have you seen how she dressed?

What a slut.

And it went on and on. Cody was livid by the time he put his phone down. He paced back and forth in his sterile, empty home.

"This is all my fault."

Why the hell did he think he could help Hannah infiltrate the Goldens?

Sure he'd been one of them. But in the time he'd been away he'd quickly forgotten how ruthless they were. They would never accept her. And now that he'd practically drawn a target on her back by pretending to date her, he'd ensure that the last few weeks of high school would probably destroy her.

"Not this time."

He'd be damned if he let those bastards destroy another innocent life. Cody blamed the Goldens and their stupid secret parties for tearing him and Elena apart. That's where they'd been the night of their stupid fight. The night they'd gotten drunk and said all kinds of things they couldn't take back. The night she'd died.

Cody picked up his phone and texted Bianca. Then he'd taken a long shower and plotted revenge. When he'd gotten out his phone was buzzing with texts.

One from Bianca.

One from Hannah.

Texts he could handle. But then she called. And her sincere voice sent shivers through him. He was right back in the fitting room. Hannah half naked, doe eyes staring up at him after their electrifying kiss, asking if she was good enough. *Shit!* He needed to get her out of his head. The *last* thing he needed was to go feeling something for a girl like Hannah. He needed to get off the phone.

He'd been harsh with her. But that was the only way this was going to work. Cody needed to stay disconnected.

CHAPTER
15

The next morning Hannah skipped up the massive stone steps to Cody's house wearing one of her new, and ridiculously expensive, workout outfits courtesy of Bianca's fine taste and Cody's deep wallet. Underneath it—her lacey LA PERLA lingerie clung to her skin like it was designed for her body alone. Hannah had to admit, maybe there was something to paying an obscene amount for clothing. Because she currently felt like she could conquer anything!

She rang the doorbell with confidence. When the butler answered, she smiled brightly. "Good morning."

"Here for Master Cody?"

"Yes. I'll show myself to his room."

It seemed all Cody needed was a good night's sleep because he was in a great mood when Hannah waltzed into his room. Fresh out of the shower, he was wearing nothing but a towel. Hannah's eyes darted straight to his glistening abs, following the sculpted V-shape muscles that disappeared beneath the towel.

"Doll face!" he exclaimed when she walked in. "You look ravishing."

"Well you're in a good mood this morning."

"Well it's a beautiful day for extortion." Cody's said giving her a dazzling smile that carved dimples into his cheeks. "And besides, why wouldn't I be in a fantastic mood with you in my life?"

Despite his sarcasm Cody's gorgeous features made Hannah's nerves flutter. "I don't know, maybe because the last time I saw you, you couldn't get away from me fast enough. And you were rude on the phone last night."

"You can't expect everyone to be as perfect as you, Hannah."

"What's that supposed to mean?"

"Don't worry about it. My head's in the game. Now we better get going, doll face," he added in an exaggeratedly snooting voice. "We don't want to be late for tennis." He smirked pulling the towel from his waist to tousle his hair.

Hannah got an eye full of Cody and tried to stifle her shock as she ran from his room.

"Meet you in the car," he called after her not even trying to suppress his laughter.

⸻

Hannah sat in the car trying to regain her composure. *What was Cody's deal?* He was like Jekyll and Hyde. She'd never encountered someone with so many mood swings. Maybe it was because of his drinking problem. *Had he fallen off the wagon again?* She hadn't wanted to bring it up, but if it was going to get in the way of her success it needed to be addressed.

Cody slid into the passenger seat of Hannah's car and frowned. "Pull up to the garage," he ordered.

"Why?"

Cody arched his eyebrow and sighed in exacerbation.

"Fine," Hannah grumbled.

She drove past the house to a two-story, six-bay garage. It was bigger than Hannah's house! Cody hopped out and punched a code into the keypad and one of the doors soundlessly slid open. He disappeared inside and then popped out dangling a set of keys.

"You don't have a license," Hannah reminded him.

"Yes, but you do," he smiled. "Park that rust bucket behind the garage. You're driving my car."

"W—"

"Because being seen in your car isn't doing either of us any favors."

Hannah begrudgingly parked her old Volvo behind the garage in the plentiful parking. By the time she lugged her backpack and tennis gear around front, Cody had pulled his car out.

Hannah nearly dropped her bags at the sight of Cody sitting in the passenger seat of his purring black Range Rover. The windows were down and he was chewing on the corner of his sunglasses as the early morning sunlight flickered across his chiseled features. He looked like he was modeling for a photo shoot.

Focus, Hannah!

Cody popped the hatch and Hannah threw her bags in the back of the SUV and an eerie thought crept into her mind. *Had Elena ridden in this car?* She knew it wasn't the car she'd died in. The news had repeatedly flashed images of the totaled sports car. *Perhaps if they'd been driving this car, Elena would still be alive.* It was built like a tank.

She slipped into the driver's seat and the soft leather upholstery seemed to wrap around her. Cody reached across and hit a button on her door. Hannah's seat smoothly repositioned her so she could reach the pedals.

"Wow. The car knows how to adjust to its driver?" Hannah asked, impressed.

A darkness fell over Cody's handsome features. "No. Those were Elena's settings."

"Oh."

"Just hold down the program button and it'll reset to remember you."

She did as she was told, but Cody's pleasant mood had evaporated, filling the car with awkward tension. Hannah hated that she'd hit a sore spot with Cody again. He'd seemed like he was actually willing to play along this morning until she'd pissed him off with her questions. *Well, since he was already mad . . .*

"About yesterday," Hannah started. "I'm sorry about drinking in front of you. That was insensitive."

"Why?"

"Because of your problem. I was drinking champagne before I kissed you and that was thoughtless. It won't happen again."

Hannah could feel Cody staring at her. And then he burst into hysterical laughter.

"Hannah, do you think your *champagne kisses* are some sort of kryptonite?"

"I don't want to be the cause of a relapse."

Cody snorted. "I don't have a drinking problem."

"Isn't that what people who have drinking problems say?"

"I wasn't at rehab for drinking!" Cody grumbled.

"Then for what?"

"Hannah, enough with the twenty questions!" Cody shouted. "You're the one who needs my help. Let's focus on your problems, not mine."

Hannah pulled over and turned on Cody. "You're right. I'm the one in charge of this relationship and I would appreciate if you would treat me with respect."

"You're twisted if you think this is a relationship, Hannah. You're blackmailing me to go to a party."

"You agreed to help me. Are you going back on your word?"

Cody stared at her, hard, as if he was trying to make up his mind. "No. But I'm renegotiating."

"What does that mean?"

"It means this is now a partnership, not your dictatorship. It's the only way this works and we *both* get what we want?"

"And what is it that you want, Cody?"

"Don't worry. It won't get in the way of your plans."

"I'm not comfortable helping you accomplish something that you won't tell me about."

"Take it or leave it, Hannah."

"I'm not bluffing. I'll report your actual test scores."

Cody shrugged.

"Fine!" Hannah put the car in gear and continued their drive to school in silence. She didn't care what Cody's motives were, as long as she got what she wanted.

What did he want?

Cody asked himself that question over and over during their silent drive to Stanton. He thought he wanted to stick it to the Goldens. To find a way to get back at them for how they'd treated him and Elena, and for what they were saying about Hannah behind her back. He'd been so angry last night. *What gave them the right to treat people the way they did?* He refused to stand by and watch the Goldens ruin another life. He wanted to protect Hannah. But the more time he spent with her the more confused he became. Maybe Hannah didn't need protecting. She was fearless and stubborn. She wasn't the least bit intimidated by him. In fact, she challenged him, and it was infuriating.

He actually enjoyed slamming tennis balls at her during their morning practice session. It was a great way to get his frustrations out. He even returned a few serves shocking the hell out of her.

"Not bad for a basketball player, huh?" he teased.

"Former," she replied.

"Bad sportsmanship isn't a good look on you."

Hannah rolled her eyes and fired a shot at his head.

Cody nailed it and whooped in celebration. "That's three in a row."

"Are you keeping score?"

"Yeah, aren't you?"

She didn't reply.

"That's three more questions you have to answer."

"Clock's ticking."

"Tell me about your family. Do you have any siblings?"

"No. It's just me and Dad."

"Hmm."

"What?"

"Sorta explains why you're a robot without a girly bone in your body."

This time it was Hannah who closed up. She dropped the ball she'd been about to serve and stomped over to her bag, shoving her racket in and slinging it over her shoulder.

"Where ya going?"

"I've had enough practice for this morning."

"I was just kidding. Well sort of, but come on. If you can dish it you gotta be able to take it."

"I can. Insult me all you want, Cody. But leave my family out of it." She stormed away heading for the locker rooms.

CHAPTER
16

Cody was leaning against his car waiting for Hannah—annoyed that she had the keys and he was locked out. *What the hell was taking her so long?* He was about to barge into the locker room to move her along when a girl walked out. He did a double take, drinking in the long stems, high heels, short skirt and tailored top. Cody barely recognized her. Hannah looked like Golden royalty—and it made him shiver.

Hannah strutted across the parking lot looking like a plastic version of herself. She'd spent way too much time in the locker room slathering on every cosmetic in the bag from Neiman Marcus. She was no Roderick or Hector, but she still managed to achieve the desired look. She wore her new blazer, shirt and stilettos along with pieces of her Stanton uniform.

Cody's face wore a look of worry when she walked up to him.

Hannah immediately doubted herself and looked down to see if she'd missed a button or something. "What?" she asked. "Did I screw something up?"

"No." Cody cleared his throat and snapped out of whatever thoughts he'd been lost in. "You look fine."

He reached for Hannah's bags and helped her stow them in the back of the Range Rover.

"Remember what I said," Cody reminded when they drove to the student lot. "The Goldens are going to want gossip from the source so you have to be prepared."

"I know, I know. Tell them I felt bad for you, you're a charity project, blah, blah, blah."

"It's important that they think you don't like me."

"That shouldn't be too hard," Hannah said smiling sweetly. "You did spend all morning insulting me. I'll just think of that."

Cody smiled. "I was just reinforcing my point."

Cody made Hannah park in the back corner of the bustling student parking lot.

"I don't want anyone to scratch it," he reasoned buffing an invisible spot off the hood with his sleeve.

"At least when we drive my car we can park anywhere we want," Hannah taunted.

"You're right, doll face," Cody said slinging an arm over her shoulder as they walked toward the school. "Your car is much better. I mean it rides so nice and the paint job is very specific. Rust chic was the look you were going for, right?"

"Hey! You're the one that said it draws attention," she ribbed, ducking out from under his arm. "I thought that was our goal?"

"Yes. But I believe I clearly said it drew the wrong kind of attention."

"Yeah, well—"

"Look out!" Cody shouted grabbing Hannah's arm and yanking her out of the path of a speeding Mercedes.

She dropped her bag and the sound of screeching brakes filled the air as she clung to Cody's chest. She could feel his heart pounding against hers as he steadied her on her feet. *Good Lord, she'd almost been hit. Cody saved her life!*

He was frantically running his hands over her, as if in disbelief that she was unharmed.

"I'm okay," she whispered, wanting to quiet the panic in his eyes.

The driver of the silver Mercedes coupe rolled down his window and hung his head out, slowly removing his sunglasses. It was Harrison Cohl.

Hannah looked back at Cody and his panic had morphed to rage as he charged toward the Mercedes.

"Jesus, Harrison! Watch where the fuck you're going!" Cody yelled.

A crowd of onlookers was gathering.

Harrison looked right through Cody to Hannah. "You okay, lovely?" he asked smoothly.

She nodded.

Harrison winked. "No harm, no foul," he purred to Cody.

"You could have killed her," Cody hissed.

"Yes, and then you'd have two dead girlfriends," he whispered. "You really should be more careful," Harrison said giving Cody a chilling grin before driving away.

Hannah, slowly approached Cody. He was visibly shaken. "Come on," she whispered slipping her hand in his and pulling him away from the crowd of students in the parking lot. "I think we've gotten enough attention."

CHAPTER

17

Hannah reassured Cody for the thousandth time that she was okay before he agreed to leave her in the library. She didn't have class until after lunch and since discovering her laptop had smashed after she dropped it to avoid getting hit by Harrison's car, the library was the only place Hannah could get any work done. Not actual schoolwork—she'd been done for weeks. But she was busy studying her tennis opponent for her match on Saturday.

She'd been alone for less then five minutes before Madison Carmichael approached her. "Hannah, right?"

Hannah nodded.

"I heard what happened this morning! Are you okay?"

"Yes. I'm fine, but my laptop wasn't so lucky."

"Oh no. Do you need a new one? I'd be happy to let you borrow mine."

Hannah looked skeptically at the gorgeous brunette. She was even prettier up close. "Thanks for the offer, but I just signed this one out from the school."

"Oh, right," Madison said looking at the laptop like a moron. "I love your blazer," she added, sitting down at Hannah's table. "I never noticed how cute you dressed before."

Hannah shrugged. Madison apparently interpreted it to mean she could ask more questions.

"So did Cody Matthews really save you?"

"Yeah. I guess he did."

"Are you two . . . dating?" Madison asked.

"I don't like to put labels on things."

Hannah smiled to herself, thinking Cody would laugh if he heard her quoting him. "The truth is I just feel bad for the guy."

Madison snorted. "Yeah, he's a total fuck up."

Hannah cringed at the cruelty in Madison's voice. She nodded. "Yeah, I guess. But he just follows me around like a lost puppy."

"I get it," Madison said. "He *is* hot. But just be careful. Hanging around with Cody isn't good for your reputation."

"I know. I was going to ditch him already but I'm sort of just using him for his key to the masquerade."

Madison's mouth fell open. "Harrison's party?"

"That's the one."

"Really?" A grin snaked across Madison's pretty face. "Ya know, I could probably get you your own key. Then you wouldn't have to drag Cody's dead weight around."

"Oh, I don't want you to go through any trouble."

"No trouble at all," Madison said, standing.

"You said what?" Cody growled from their spot on the lawn.

"I did what you said. Why are you getting so mad?" Hannah asked taking a swig of the vanilla latte Cody bought her for lunch from their private campus kiosk.

"I didn't tell you to mention our plan!"

"The best lie is a true one."

"What?"

"If I can get my own key to the party, then I won't have to sneak in using yours. It means that they'll want me there. That's the whole point of this. Making actual friends and memories in my last few weeks of school."

"Hannah, I hate to break it to you, but you don't just dress pretty one day and get invited into the Goldens inner circle. They're up to something."

"Like what?"

"I don't know, but I think we're about to find out."

Harrison Cohl was sauntering toward them looking like he'd just walked out of a GQ ad. "Hannah, darling. I just heard your laptop was damaged in our little run in this morning. Is this true?"

"Well . . . I mean . . . yes, but," she blushed, realizing she was stammering like an idiot.

"Well that won't do. What's your home address? I'll send a replacement over today."

"Oh, that's not necessary. I have a computer at home. And my father always has extras laying around."

"Nonsense. I own up to my responsibilities." Harrison said glaring at Cody. "Where shall I send your new laptop?"

"She said she doesn't want anything from you," Cody growled.

"Does he always speak for you?" Harrison asked looking at Hannah with concern.

Hannah glared at Cody. "No, I make my own decisions."

"Good. You see, Cody, I'm simply dealing with my indiscretions like a gentleman. When you break something, you should offer to repair it. Not get it drunk and drive it into a tree."

Cody snapped. He was on his feet in an instant. He had Harrison by the throat, rammed against the trunk of the massive oak they'd been sitting under. Harrison held his arms up in surrender, as Hannah tried uselessly to pull Cody away before he got himself expelled.

"You don't get to talk about her," Cody growled, fury radiated off him in waves.

"Or, what? You'll kill me too?"

"Stop it!" Hannah yelled, finally shoving her way between them.

She kept one hand on Cody's heaving chest while Harrison smoothed out his blazer.

"Be careful, Hannah. I'd hate to see him ruin another sweet girl."

Harrison shook his head and walked away, as the rest of the campus stared at Hannah and Cody—cell phones out to capture the whole embarrassing scene.

No chance the Goldens didn't know who Hannah was now.

CHAPTER
18

Cody grabbed his bag and stormed to the parking lot. He needed to get the hell out of there or he was going to lose it. Harrison's sickening grin brought Cody back to his last night with Elena. Harrison's words echoed through Cody's head. *God I love taking things from you.* The memories made Cody see red. Harrison was the reason Cody's life was fucked right now. Deep down he knew it, but he couldn't prove it.

He kept pumping his legs trying to put distance between him and the school because he could feel it coming. His breathing was ragged, his heart racing. Cody scarcely heard Hannah's voice calling after him as he charged through the parking lot. He spotted his car and reached into his pocket. *Shit! Hannah still had the keys!*

Cody walked behind the car and leaned against it trying to calm himself down. He pressed the palms of his hands into his eye sockets until his saw spots. It wasn't helping. He could feel his muscles going rigid. He took in a shaky breath and started to list things to keep him in the present. He needed an anchor to keep him from slipping back into the nightmares of his past.

"Friday, May 12th. Calculus exam. 1:30 pm. Hannah . . ."

"Cody?" Hannah's voice drifted to his ears. He could feel her softly kneeling next to him. "What's wrong?"

"Please leave," Cody ground out through his clenched jaw.

"No. Tell me what to do."

"Hannah . . ." he begged. "Please, leave me alone."

He heard the car unlock and Hannah put her shoulder under his arm dragging him to his feet.

"Come on. Let's go," she urged.

"Where?"

"Anywhere you want."

He balled his hands into fists and tried to get his limbs to respond. He finally got in the car with Hannah's help. She raced around to the driver's side and buckled him in.

"Tell me where to go," she begged.

"I don't know," he growled.

"Pick somewhere that makes you happy and I'll drive you there, okay?"

Cody took a deep breath and closed his eyes.

"Cody!" Hannah yelled. "Open your eyes and give me directions."

His eyes flew open and he looked at the road. Hannah was already out of the school parking lot. "Hidden Hallow Drive."

"I don't know where that is. Right or left?"

"Right," Cody answered.

Hannah turned right. Her hand reached for Cody's and squeezed. "Now what?"

"Left on Powell Road. Two miles ahead."

She squeezed warmth back into his fingers and whispered, "I'm with you."

CHAPTER

19

They were sitting on the grass, their backs resting against the grill of the Range Rover staring out over the lush green pastures of the horse farm below. They hadn't spoken since they got there. Hannah sat quietly next to Cody, their shoulders touching, offering her silent support.

"How did you know what to do?" he finally asked.

"My mom used to have panic attacks."

"Why?"

"Is there a why?" Hannah asked.

Cody shrugged. "For me there is."

Hannah searched his exquisite features, waiting for him to share more. But Cody clearly seemed tormented by the idea of saying more. To save him from suffering she began talking.

"I don't know what it was for my mother. I always tried to be perfect so I wouldn't trigger her attacks. But it didn't matter if I was the perfect daughter. In the end she left us anyway. I was eight."

Cody finally looked at Hannah. It felt like he was seeing her for the first time. His brown eyes glowed—the sunlight catching the tiny flecks of gold, making them dance like fireflies. There was so much sorrow on his beautiful face that Hannah barely recognized him. "I'm sorry," he whispered, taking her hand in his.

Hannah swallowed hard, staring at Cody's hand and feeling his warmth and sincerity. "Thanks."

"It's not your fault she had panic attacks."

Hannah smiled sadly and pulled her hand away. "You don't know that."

"I do. We do it to ourselves. No one causes it. It's just our inability to sort out reality."

"I heard my mother tell my father that we made her sick." Hannah said quietly. She could feel Cody staring at her but she couldn't meet his gaze. Instead, she looked down at the ground and tore up a long blade of grass, wrapping it around her finger. She gave a sad laugh. "She couldn't stand the sight of us. And then she left us. What else am I supposed to take from that?"

Cody grabbed Hannah's hands, stilling her fidgeting. "I don't know. It was probably something between your parents, because I find it pretty hard to believe that someone couldn't stand the sight of you." He tucked a stray piece of hair behind Hannah's ear, smiling kindly.

She tried to return his smile, but her heart hurt. Hannah never spoke about her mother. She tried not to think about her at all, because all it did was make her feel inadequate.

"Thank you," Cody said softly.

"For what?"

Now it was his turn to look at the ground. "For helping me."

Hannah hated the serious tone their conversation had taken. It felt too . . . *real*. Today had gotten off track and she needed to right it. "You're welcome." Hannah nudged Cody's shoulder trying to lighten the mood. "So why this place?"

"It just makes everything better."

"That's all I get?"

"I came here after my parents got divorced."

"Oh, I'm sorry."

Cody shrugged. "It's okay. It was a long time ago."

"But how'd you even find this place? It's in the middle of nowhere."

"I used to come here when I was a kid. My parents had horses at the stables and they would let me come out here with the hounds to placate my begging for a dog of my own."

"Why couldn't you have a dog?"

Cody sighed. "Too messy."

"I can see that."

"What's that supposed to mean?"

"Well, your house is kind of . . . sterile."

"Sterile?"

"Yes. It looks like a museum. I'm actually surprised you're allowed to live there. Your room is the only thing in the house that isn't perfect and white."

Cody burst into laughter. "Please . . . don't hold back."

"Sorry," Hannah blushed.

"No. It's honestly refreshing. I hate my house. It's huge, but it's always empty. Everything has to be kept just so, but for what? It's just me and my dad. And he's never there. It makes no sense."

"The grass is always greener," Hannah sighed.

"You just called my house a sterile museum."

"Yes, but I didn't say I wouldn't live there. We can trade if you'd like. I have a dog, a cluttered house and my dad is *always* home."

Cody laughed. "Careful, I might take you up on it."

"So, it's Friday. We blew off school . . . what do you want to do for the rest of the day?" Hannah asked.

"I don't know. But going to my sterile house and being alone isn't appealing."

"Okay. How about we go to my house, play with Custard, and start my movie tutorial."

"Custard?"

"My dog."

"You named your dog Custard?"

"I was eight!"

Cody laughed and stood up, pulling Hannah with him. "It's a date."

CHAPTER
20

Their conversation was easy on the way to Hannah's house. And Cody noticed she was getting more comfortable driving the Range Rover. She even dared to open the sunroof. He smiled as he watched Hannah's hair dance about in the breeze while she animatedly told him about Custard the dog.

It seemed he'd finally found something that she was passionate about. It was the first time he'd heard her responses not sound like an automated reading of Wikipedia. He noted the adorable dimple she had in her right cheek when she laughed. He found himself absurdly jealous of the outpouring of love that Custard conjured in Hannah. He couldn't wait to meet the fur ball and size him up.

It turned out it was impossible not to like Custard. The chubby corgi greeted them at the door with excited yips and tail wagging. It was Mr. Stark that needed coaxing from Hannah.

"Dad, I'm home."

There was a muffled response from somewhere in the cluttered house.

"I brought a friend from school over."

Another muffled grunt.

"I'll be right back," Hannah said apologetically before disappearing with Custard hot on her heels. Cody couldn't help but smile as he watched the little dog jog adoringly after Hannah, his short legs tripping over the mess of wires and books that covered the living room floor.

Cody's eyes absorbed the cheerfulness of Hannah's home. It was small, but exploding with color and life. Every mismatched piece of furniture was covered with either books or framed portraits of Hannah smiling brightly back at him. There were framed diplomas, trophies and knickknacks everywhere—globes, antique clocks and model cars. Cozy blankets of different sizes and colors draped the back of the eclectic chairs and sofas, inviting him to sit and stay awhile. There seemed to be no rhyme or reason to the decorating style of the house and Cody loved it.

He was smirking and shaking his head when Hannah reappeared with two bottles of water.

"What?" she asked.

"Nothing," he replied coyly. He followed her up the stairs to her bedroom and laughed when he entered the room. "Now this is more like it."

"What's that supposed to mean?" she asked, hands on her hips.

"To see into ones room, is to see into their soul."

"That's not a quote," Hannah scoffed.

"Well it should be. I was starting to think I had you all wrong, but this room is you, down to the perfectly pressed vanilla drapes and matching comforter."

"I like order. You saw the rest of my house. It's a bit . . . busy. I find I'm most productive in a calm environment."

"You mean bland environment," Cody teased tossing the plainest beige pillow he'd ever seen at Hannah.

"Hey!"

Custard barked and promptly leaped onto the pillow making himself comfortable.

Hannah crouched down and scratched his neck before giving him a kiss on the head. "Don't you look like a little prince," she crooned in a childish voice.

"More like a fat old king," Cody joked.

Hannah mocked insult and tried to cover Custard's gigantic ears. "Don't you listen to the grouch, Custard. He's just jealous."

Custard barked in agreement and Cody laughed. "Alright, we haven't got all day. Let's get this movie marathon started."

～♀

Hannah started out taking notes, but halfway through Pretty Woman she gave up.

"I can't believe you Pretty-Womaned me at Neiman Marcus! This movie is ridiculous!"

"It's a classic," Cody argued lounging on her bed with Custard traitorously cuddled next to him. One belly rub was all it took and he'd been laying paws up next to Cody for the remainder of the movie.

"How is a prostitute falling for a rich guy a classic?"

"It's like a modern Cinderella."

Now it was Hannah's turn to throw a pillow. "This is the most chauvinistic, unlikely, degrading . . ."

"Isn't that what fairytales are?" Cody laughed.

Hannah sighed. "Yes, and I suppose that's why I'm not a fan of fairytales. But this is still a terrible movie."

"No way! I love Pretty Woman."

"Oh, please! Are you telling me if you were Richard Gere you'd fall for her?"

"She knows cars. That's hot."

Hannah rolled her eyes.

"And she's easy to talk to. Plus I like all her random facts."

"Random facts?"

"Don't think I didn't see you checking the length of your foot," Cody taunted, playfully grabbing Hannah's feet. "It's true, you know? Your foot is as long as your elbow to your wrist," he said skimming his fingers teasingly over her captive feet.

She squealed, in terror. "No!"

"Is someone ticklish?"

She shook her head fervently, but her flushed cheeks and wide eyes gave her away and Cody lunged. He and Custard ganged up on her, pinning her to the bed and ruthlessly tickling her—Custard's wet nose worming its way to her ears and neck.

"Omigod! No! Stop!" Hannah's protests and squealing laughter peeled through the room, mixed with Custard's barking and Cody's taunts.

Hannah tried to fight back but Cody wasn't nearly as ticklish and his precise attacks to her thighs and ribs turned her muscles to jelly, leaving her breathless.

Cody straddled her, knees on either side of her hips. She squirmed and he laughed, weaving his fingers with hers as she tried to fend him off. She was suddenly mesmerized by the joy on his beautiful face. This was the second time today Hannah was seeing behind the veil—the real Cody—not the dark, brooding boy he wanted the world to see.

Her heart hammered in her chest. Hannah stilled, her cheeks rosy as she gazed at her reflection in his dark eyes. Cody stopped moving too. His face was inches from hers, his warm breath mixing with hers. Cody pushed her hands above her head, their fingers still intertwined. She licked her lips, trembling at the confusing emotions racing through her.

Suddenly this didn't feel like practice. But it didn't feel wrong either.

CHAPTER

21

Hannah's shiny blonde hair was sprawled out on the bed like a crown. Cody wanted to touch it. He wanted to touch all of her. He wanted to bury himself in her beauty and drive away the remaining darkness that had tried to drown him today. But he couldn't. Not without consequences. Not without screwing everything up. But just the same, he couldn't pull himself away from Hannah either.

Watching her lick her delicate pink lips sent shockwaves straight to his core. He was losing his resolve. And then she bit her lip, looking at him with a strange mix of desire and fear. *Shit, pull away, Cody.* But he couldn't. He was transfixed in the moment, powerless to her will. *How was this beautiful creature untouched? Was that the only reason he wanted her?*

Hannah blinked as though she'd heard his thoughts and let go of his hands. *Good,* he thought. *Pull away from me, because I'm too weak to do it myself.*

But instead of pushing him off, Hannah's hands settled

on either side of Cody's face. She slid one hand into his hair making him shudder and close his eyes. Her other hand delicately traced his jaw until she reached his lips. He parted them and exhaled her name, but she swallowed his words, pressing her lips to his.

The kiss ignited a spark that threatened to combust everything around them. Cody sighed into the kiss and let go of his final ounce of restraint. He'd been holding onto his darkness for over a year and Hannah had been slowly poking holes in his armor, shining in bits of light. But it wasn't enough to sustain him. He'd had a taste and he wanted more—needed more.

Their hands chased each other, greedily stripping away the clothing keeping them apart. Cody fisted his hands in Hannah's hair, kissing her desperately. And from the way she kissed him back, it was evident that this was no longer pretend.

Shit! Stop this right now, Matthews.

But he couldn't. Not when Hannah was laying before him looking like an angel in the lingerie *he* bought her.

To conquer the world, indeed.

Cody was convinced there was no one on the planet who could resist Hannah when she was looking at him the way she was right now. *Full of hope and promises.* Cody had no doubt that if he let her, Hannah would take away his pain and self-loathing. He knew he could bury himself in her goodness for a while. *But would she be just another Band-Aid or could she really heal him? And how bad would he destroy her in the process?*

He didn't have time to contemplate. A sharp knock at the door broke them from their trance. Hannah quickly jumped to her feet and threw on an oversized sweatshirt and pajama pants that were conveniently resting on her desk chair, while Cody scrambled into his khakis and t-shirt.

＿＿♀＿

Hannah quickly checked her reflection in the mirror and smoothed her hair down. She looked at Cody who was now sitting on the bed looking a bit shell shocked. Custard was sitting at his feet wagging his tail. Hannah creaked the door open to see her father's anxious face.

"Hey, Dad."

"Everything all right up here? I thought I heard yelling."

"Yes everything's fine. Just watching movies and playing with Custard."

Her father tried to peer around her into the room. "Dad, do we have any popcorn?" she asked distracting him from the disheveled appearance of her bed. "We need movie snacks."

"Yes. The air pop is in the pantry."

"Great! Can you help me get it down," she asked, moving into the hall and tugging her father with her. He nodded distractedly. "Cody, queue up the next film, I'll be back in a minute," she called over her shoulder, desperately hoping he'd still be there when she got back to her room. The haunted look on his face the moment before her father interrupted them worried her.

CHAPTER

22

Cody paced Hannah's room and chastised himself for letting things go too far. *Get it together, Matthews.* Today had snowballed. The best thing he could do was leave and pretend it never happened. Denial—that was something he was good at, something he was prepared for. Unlike this . . . whatever this was. He rubbed his face in frustration. *How the hell had Hannah Stark disarmed him?*

He needed to leave before things got even more out of hand. Cody moved around the room collecting his articles of discarded clothing. He found his tie lying across Hannah's desk. He marched over to snag it and glanced at the open notebook it was resting on. Cody blinked in disbelief as he read Hannah's scrawling penmanship on the page.

Keep your eyes on the prize.
1. Get the key.
2. Get the guy.

3. *Make memories.*
4. *Give epic graduation speech.*
5. *Check high school perfection off my* résumé.
"Practice makes perfect."

He snorted. "And she thinks fairytales are fucked up."

Maybe Cody was wrong. Hannah didn't feel anything, she was just using him. *That was their deal, after all.* He sighed, his mind mingled with a mix of disappointment and relief. He needed to get over it. Whatever moment he thought he had with Hannah hadn't been real. And it didn't matter—he wouldn't let her matter.

After Elena, he vowed not to let anyone in again. *So what if Hannah was using him. At least she was upfront about it.* Cody had used plenty of people. This was probably just karmic payback. *Besides, wasn't he using her too?* Playing their twisted game was better than facing the dark pain that came crashing in whenever he was alone.

Cody looked back at the notebook and smirked. Maybe they could both get what they wanted. She could be his distraction and he could be her whipping boy.

$$\sim_{\heartsuit}\backsim$$

Hannah padded back into the room with a huge bowl of popcorn and Custard at her heels.

"Sorry," she grimaced once she'd closed the door. "I told you, my dad is *always* here."

Cody shrugged. "I ordered pizza," he said without looking up from his phone.

"Oh. Okay."

Hannah studied Cody for signs of the boy she'd been kissing earlier. But it was obvious he was gone—once again replaced with an aloof imposter. She sighed, telling herself it was better this way.

"Shall we continue with your education?" Cody asked, finally putting his phone down and looking at her with his piercing dark eyes.

He was sitting on her bed in his soft gray t-shirt and rumpled khakis, his feet bare. *How was it possible to look so casual and sexy at once?* Cody threaded his hands behind his head, exposing his perfect abs and Hannah swallowed hard.

"Um, I don't think that's such a good idea with my dad here."

Cody smirked. "I was talking about the movie," he said gesturing to the television with the remote and pressing play. "Besides, you're showing improvement. You can cross kissing and foreplay off your list. I guess practice really does make perfect, doesn't it?" he mocked.

Hannah hated the haughty detached tone of Cody's voice. But what had she expected? That's why she'd chosen him. He was a grade-A asshole. Well that and he's the only one she had enough leverage over to blackmail. Sure, they'd shared a rare moment of companionability and even chemistry, but that's all it was—a fluke, probably brought on by the post-endorphins of his panic attack.

"I told you I was a quick study," Hannah quipped grabbing her notebook and climbing onto her bed. "What's up next?"

"Cruel Intentions."

Hannah shook off the eerie feeling the movie title envoked and called Custard up to sit between them. Going forward, a barrier would be necessary. Caring about Cody Matthews wouldn't help Hannah achieve her goals.

CHAPTER

23

Hannah enjoyed the twisted teen film more than she'd expected. It was better than Pretty Woman at least. But Cody was notably agitated. Perhaps watching the love interest get killed by a car hit too close to home. Hannah felt bad, but then she reminded herself to keep her feelings out of it.

"So do girls really do that?" she asked when it was over. "Practice kissing and sex with each other?"

"I don't know, Hannah. You're the girl."

"Yes, I am a girl. But I'm normal. I need you to tell me what's normal for the Goldens."

"They do a lot of fucked up things. This movie is basically their anthem, and I don't mean the ending where they all wake up and feel bad for the shit they've done. They're conniving assholes who get off on power and manipulation. You should fit right in," he muttered gathering his things.

"That's uncalled for, Cody. We have a deal."

"Yes, I know. You won't let me forget it."

"Well where are you going? I thought we were going to watch Mean Girls and Can't Hardly Wait?"

"I'm done for today. We can pick it up tomorrow."

"I have my tennis match tomorrow," Hannah called after him.

Cody was already out the front door when Hannah caught up to him. "Wait, I have to drive you."

"It's a mile, Hannah. I think I can handle it."

"But my car's at your house."

He was already in the driver's seat. "I'll pick you up tomorrow."

"Oh so you're taking me to my tennis match at the crack of dawn?" she taunted.

Cody sighed and slumped his head against the steering wheel before finally unbuckling his seatbelt. He slid out and walked around to the passenger seat, grumbling the whole way.

"Can you give me a minute to change?" Hannah begged. "I'm sort of in my pajamas."

Cody flicked his wrist dismissively without looking at her and Hannah retreated to switch her plaid pajama bottoms for yoga pants. She swooped her hair up in a messy bun and stuffed her feet into her favorite converse before jogging out to the Range Rover.

Cody's head was in his hands when she approached. Hannah picked up her pace worried he was having another panic attack.

"You okay?" she asked when she got in.

"Fine," Cody grumbled rubbing his temples.

"Are you sure?"

"I'm not that fragile, Hannah," Cody barked. "Can you just drive me home and retrieve your car?"

Hannah almost made it the short drive to Cody's without caving in, but the flashbacks of her mother's depression and panic attacks pulled at her heartstrings. She knew Cody wasn't fine. Hannah was sensitive to the signs. Agitation, mood swings, deep breathing, shaking, headaches . . . He'd displayed them all on the drive. She refused to do nothing and let this sickness steal someone else.

"Cody, I know the movie upset you. We can talk about it if it'll help."

"It won't."

Good, he admitted he was upset at least. "I bet I'm cheaper than your therapist," she grinned trying to lighten the mood.

"Let it go, Hannah."

"No, Cody. You can't keep things bottled up. That's what my mom did and—"

"I'm not your mother!" he yelled.

"I know that. And I'm trying to make sure you don't become her."

Cody stared at her with anger and confusion as Hannah pulled into his driveway and parked.

"I lied okay. My mom didn't just leave. She killed herself! She took a bath with a bottle of pills and left us a sweet little note that said she needed to leave."

Cody's eyes were wide and full of pain. "I'm sorry," he said softly.

"Don't be sorry. Be better than she was. You can't leave your problems behind. You need to deal with them or they'll drown you."

Cody shook his head and Hannah could see his self-loathing.

She put her hands on his cheeks and gripped his face hard making him look at her. "Cody, you're not a lost cause."

His face was so close to hers she could feel his breath. When Hannah looked at him she saw the boy he kept hidden. The one who still possessed goodness. He leaned his forehead against hers and for a moment they both held their breath, shouldering each other's pain.

When Cody opened his eyes, they were dark. He caught a tear from Hannah's cheek. "Some people aren't worth saving," he whispered slipping from her grasp and exiting the car.

He was up the stone steps, disappearing into the house before she even turned the car off. Hannah swiped the tears from her face, angry that thoughts of her mother still held such power over her.

Cody was wrong. He was worth saving. *But what could she do? He wasn't hers to save.* Hannah trudged to her car and drove home in echoing silence, with only her melancholy thoughts to keep her company.

CHAPTER
24

When Hannah arrived back home her dad was waiting and he didn't look happy.

"Were you driving a Range Rover when you left?"

"Yes. It's Cody's."

"I don't want you driving someone else's vehicle, Hannah."

"He doesn't have a license, Dad."

Hannah's father looked perplexed. "Do I even want to know?"

She hated lying to her father. It was their one rule. He was analytical and never really overreacted or got upset about things. He just wanted to be accurately informed.

"Dad, do you remember hearing about Cody Matthews in the news?"

He shook his head.

"He got in that car accident . . . and his girlfriend died."

Her father's eyes grew with recognition. "They were students at your school."

"Yes. Cody still is."

"Hannah, I don't like this."

"Dad, it's not a big deal. We're working on a project together for school and I've offered to give him rides since he can't drive. We took his car today, but I won't do it again if you don't want me to."

Her father cut his eyes suspiciously at her. "And what about, H?" he asked. "Is he part of this *school project?*"

"H?"

Her father picked up a white box that Hannah missed amongst the daily clutter of items waiting to be carried up the stairs. It was a Macbook Air, with red handwriting scrawled across the top of the box. *Problem solved. Call me if you need anything else – H.* A phone number was scribbled beneath the note along with a tiny heart.

Hannah looked at her father's suspicious glare and groaned. *This was precisely why she'd asked Harrison NOT to send her a laptop.*

"Dad, I told him I didn't need it."

"Who's it from?"

"Harrison Cohl."

That was a name he *did* know. Hannah's father provided the Cohl's security software for their computer. Well at least he used to, before they'd been elected to government positions. Losing their account had been a big hit to his business.

"Is he mocking your computer?" he asked in astonishment. "Because I can tell you right now, it's far superior to this toy!" he muttered waving the Macbook around.

"No! Dad. I bumped into Harrison in the parking lot today and dropped my laptop. The screen smashed and he feels like it was his fault so he offered to get me a new one.

I told him it wasn't necessary," Hannah replied trying to soothe her father's uncharacteristic hostility. "He's just trying to be nice."

"We don't need his charity."

"I know, Dad. I'm going to call him and return it, okay?"

Her father nodded and handed Hannah the slim white box. "Please do."

Hannah sighed as she watched her father disappear back into his study. *Today was not her day.* She trudged up the stairs with the Macbook, already typing Harrison's number into her phone and shooting him a text.

THANKS FOR THE LAPTOP.
IT WAS VERY GENEROUS.
BUT I CAN'T ACCEPT.

Hannah paused before hitting send. She couldn't piss Harrison off if she still hoped to get an invite to his party. She added to her text message.

MY FATHER ALREADY REPLACED IT.
DON'T WANT TO HURT HIS FEELINGS.
BUT THANK YOU – HANNAH

An immediate response came through.

AT LEAST KEEP MY NUMBER ;-) – HARRISON

Hannah blushed and texted back a smiley face.

GLAD I BUMPED INTO YOU – HARRISON

She laughed. *Bumped?* Well that was one way to look at it.

LOL – HANNAH

CALL IF YOU NEED ME – HARRISON

OK – HANNAH.

Hannah shook her head at the strangeness of her day. She'd finally gotten Harrison's attention. It wasn't how she'd planned it, but she could adjust. The important thing was he knew who she was and seemed to be flirting with her! Now that she had his number she could talk to him without his Golden army watching—judging. If she watched enough rom-coms she should be able to charm the pants off him. She had Harrison right where she wanted him. High school perfection was in sight!

So why was it that she couldn't stop thinking about Cody?

She couldn't shake the nagging feeling that he was hurting and she was probably the only one who knew, or cared. Hannah picked up her phone and tapped out a quick message. Yes, she knew Cody wasn't her actual boyfriend, but he was still human and she refused to sit by and let him suffer silently. She knew too well what that felt like.

JUST CHECKING IN – HANNAH

After ten minutes of relentlessly checking her phone, Hannah, tapped out another text. She tried a different approach this time since Cody apparently preferred denial rather than dealing with his issues.

DO YOU WANT TO COME TO MY TENNIS MATCH TOMORROW? – HANNAH

Relief flooded her when she saw the text bubble pop up. *Had she really thought he'd harm himself?* Perhaps she was overreacting, but that was par for the course when suicide runs in your family.

IS IT A BOYFRIEND DUTY? – CODY

NO. IT'S A FRIEND DUTY – HANNAH

WE'RE NOT FRIENDS – CODY

His words stung, but she knew he'd meant them to. Hannah fleetingly thought Cody would be a worthy chess opponent. He had a tactical mind. But she wasn't pushed away so easily.

COME ON. DON'T BE A SHEEP – HANNAH

She smirked at her clever retort, knowing he'd be proud she was quoting Cruel Intentions.

I HAVE PLANS – CODY

LIAR – HANNAH

Hannah finally gave up when there was no response after an hour. She flopped into bed and turned the light off, determined not to let her boy trouble consume her dreams.

CHAPTER
25

Now this was some karmic crap! Hannah rubbed her hands together to keep warm before trying the ignition again. Another cold front had rolled through over night and the app on her phone said it was currently 39 degrees! *Her car hated the cold almost as much as she did.* She said a silent prayer and turned the keys again only to be met with a weak clicking sound.

"Great! Just great!"

Hannah checked the time. Her dad would almost be in New York by now. He left at dawn to drive to a conference for the weekend. She hated to call him. He worried enough as it was, and after the drama with Cody and Harrison yesterday he'd been hesitant to leave her at all. Hannah grabbed her bag and ran inside to get out of the cold while she tried to solve her issue of finding a ride to her tennis match. She could call a cab, but it would be expensive. The match was almost an hour away. Hannah mentally calculated the fare there and back and frowned. *Cody it was.* She dialed his number—there wasn't time for their text chess games this morning.

Cody answered on the first ring. His voice low . . . short. She was surprised he was even awake this early.

"Hannah?"

"Hey."

"What do you want?"

"Can you pretty please take me to tennis this morning? I—"

Hannah's words dropped off when she heard a female voice calling Cody's name in the background. Cody's muffled voice spoke away from the phone, assuring whoever was with him that he'd, '*be right there.*'

"This isn't a good time, Hannah. I told you I have plans."

Then he disconnected, leaving Hannah dazed and deflated.

She took a deep breath and collected herself. She couldn't be mad. Cody wasn't her *real* boyfriend. He was allowed to see other girls. And to be fair he'd said he was busy today. Maybe he'd actually sought help last night in the form of a friend? *Or more than a friend,* Hannah thought recalling the sultry sound of the girl's voice. *Ugh, what did it matter?* Hannah didn't have time to worry about Cody and their messed up games. She needed to get to her tennis match.

Her eyes settled on the white Macbook box on the foyer table. *Perhaps fate was smiling on her after all.*

Hannah dialed another number while nervously chewing her lip.

Harrison's sleep husked voice answered after several rings. "-lo?"

"Harrison? It's Hannah. Stark."

"Hannah?"

"Yes, I'm sorry to call so early, but you said if I ever needed anything . . . if that offer's still good, I would really love to take you up on it right now."

Hannah had a strange sensation Harrison was smiling on the other end of the phone when she relayed her failed attempts to get to her tennis match. He agreed to drive her and said he'd be there in twenty minutes.

⟨♡⟩

Hannah heard tires on gravel and glanced at her watch. *Harrison was prompt.* She collected her tennis bags and rackets, grabbing the Macbook as she locked the house behind her. She nearly dropped her bags along with her jaw when she caught sight of the slick black limo in her driveway. The window lowered and Harrison grinned out at her.

"Morning!" he called raising a champagne flute and flashing a devious smile. "Ready, Ace?"

The driver swiftly stowed Hannah's bags and ushered her into the limo. The rich leather interior was warm and inviting, just like Harrison's smile. Hannah's skin tingled with nervous excitement. She'd never been in a limo before. And with the door shut and partition raised she felt a bit like a caged animal—a lion and a lamb.

Harrison slid closer to Hannah and offered her a champagne flute. "May I *serve* you?"

"Thank you, but I can't drink before a match."

"It's only orange juice."

Hannah raised her eyebrow suspiciously.

"Oh, mine's a mimosa. But don't worry, I brought another bottle for later so we can celebrate your certain victory."

Hannah took the orange juice and sniffed the glass tentatively, while Harrison studied her.

"My, my, aren't we distrustful. But I guess that's to be expected when you spend so much time with Cody Matthews. You probably have to police his drinking habit, don't you?" Harrison leaned in. "Don't worry. I'm nothing like him. I can handle my liquor and if not," he winked, "I have a driver."

He clinked glasses with Hannah and downed his mimosa.

"What do you see in him anyway?" Harrison asked refilling his glass.

"I don't really want to discuss Cody right now."

"That's right, he stood you up." Harrison gave another wolfish grin. "Well, his folly is my fortune."

Hannah nearly snorted. "I have a feeling he won't be happy I got a ride from you."

"You don't need his permission to talk to me, Hannah. We're just friends, aren't we?" Harrison asked, taking her hand. But the way he caressed it and the sinister twinkle in his eye told her Harrison wore a mask just like Cody did. But warning bells went off in Hannah's head when Harrison touched her, telling her his mask hid things far darker than Cody's.

It suddenly felt like there wasn't enough air in the car. Hannah rolled down the window and let the biting cold clear her mind. She needed to change the subject.

"I wanted to thank you for the laptop, but I brought it with me to return to you."

"I don't mind replacing it."

"I know, but my father—"

"Yes, yes. You already mentioned he replaced it," Harrison said waving away her argument, "But I still don't see why you can't keep both."

"I really can't. Computers are sort of his thing. He'd be hurt."

"What about my feelings?"

Hannah smiled. "I think you'll be just fine. You're tougher than you look."

"Hey!" Harrison mocked insult and playfully nudged her shoulder with his. "That's what everyone thinks, you know? That I'm rich and spoiled and without feelings."

"I don't think that?" Hannah replied worrying she'd actually insulted him.

"Good." He smiled and tucked Hannah's arm under his.

Harrison was staring at her, his blue eyes piercing hers hungrily. He ran a finger down her cheek and she shivered. "I'm so grateful I didn't harm you in the parking lot. I feel terrible about it. Please let me make it up to you."

"Honestly, Harrison. It wasn't a big deal. And you're making it up to me right now."

Harrison pouted. "Giving you a ride hardly makes us square." His blue eyes twinkled, luring her in. "Let me take you on a date."

Hannah swallowed, she'd suddenly forgotten how to speak. This was what she wanted. *Wasn't it? A date with Harrison Cohl.* If she could pull this off she could get her own key to the ball!

Harrison took her silence as rejection.

"Forgive me. I was hoping you and Cody weren't that serious, but . . ." he sighed. "I know it's not my place to say so, but you can do much better than Cody Matthews. He doesn't have a good reputation."

"I know all about his reputation," Hannah said a bit too defensively.

Harrison smiled. "Of course."

"What do you have against him? I thought you used to be friends?"

"We were. But that was before I realized how reckless Cody is. I just don't want to see you get hurt, Hannah."

"I'm not foolish enough to let someone like Cody hurt me."

"That's what Elena thought," Harrison said quietly.

"What?"

"I'm sorry. I shouldn't have said anything. It's just . . ." Harrison trailed off.

"What?"

"She came to me about Cody. The day of the accident they'd had a terrible fight. She was covered in bruises, Hannah. Elena was terrified of him. I never should have let them leave together. If only I'd done more. I . . . Hannah, I vowed not to sit by the next time."

A cavern of emptiness carved a home in Hannah's chest. *Could Cody really have hurt Elena?* He still seemed so wrecked by her loss. And in the few glimpses she'd gotten of Cody, he'd shown her a gentle vulnerability that she never would have suspected was capable of violence. Hannah suddenly saw the massive flaw in her plans. She'd taken both Cody and Harrison at face value and now found herself among monsters.

"Hannah, please keep this to yourself. I've never shared it with anyone."

"You didn't tell the police?"

"I didn't see the point. It wouldn't change anything.

Elena was dead and Cody was arrested. And honestly, I was ashamed."

"But your family helped Cody? Their lawyers got him a slap on the wrist!"

"Like you said, we used to be friends, Hannah. It's hard when someone you care about betrays you."

It certainly is, she thought, biting her lip to hold back the tears. *How had she not seen through Cody's lies?* Hannah had felt bad for him—losing his girlfriend, abandoned by his friends, disowned by his team. But he'd done it all to himself.

"Promise me you won't tell anyone. Especially Cody. He's not stable, Hannah. If he hurt you because of something I said . . ." Harrison turned toward her, moving closer. His eyes were shining and his fingers trembled as he touched her cheek pulling them even closer together. Their foreheads touched and Hannah held her breath. *Was Harrison going to kiss her?* "Please, Hannah. Promise you won't say anything. I couldn't deal with it, if he hurt you."

"I promise," she whispered.

Her phone buzzed in her lap and they jumped apart, the spell broken.

Hannah looked down to see, *Dad*, flash across the screen. She scrambled to answer it. "Hey, Dad."

"Hi, honey. Just checking to see if you made it to your match."

"Almost there."

"Are you still driving?"

"Yep."

"You're not supposed to be on the phone while you drive."

"I wouldn't if you weren't calling," she reminded jokingly.

"Okay. Just text me when you get there. I love you, Hannah."

"Love you too, Dad."

Hannah disconnected and felt her cheeks flush, slightly embarrassed that Harrison witnessed her dorky display of affection with her father.

"Sorry about that. He worries."

"It's sweet," Harrison replied genuinely. "My parents could take a lesson from your father." He reached for her hand. "So tell me about this tennis match."

CHAPTER
26

Cody stuffed his hands in his pockets and sunk further into the stiff collar of his wool peacoat. The frigid morning air turned his cheeks red and his fingers stiff. Although his body shivered against the cold, Cody welcomed the numbing feeling. He only wished it could reach his heart.

Staring at Elena's tombstone always crippled him, but it was something he made himself do. Cody was under the impression that if he could desensitize himself to the pain, it would go away. But it'd been over a year and every time he visited her grave he felt like the world was caving in beneath him. He stared at the single white rose he'd placed under her headstone's inscription.

Elena Harlow Michaels
1999 – 2016
"Death leaves a heartache no one can heal,
love leaves a memory no one can steal."

The words gutted him. They summed up his ruined life in one perfect sentence. He felt the darkness come, swift and consuming as he struggled to force himself to breathe. Sometimes he wished his body would give up and he would just collapse and lay there next to Elena for eternity. But whenever he tried to give in to the temptation, his heart remembered the pain she'd inflicted and how she'd selfishly left Cody alone with her betrayal and no one left to be angry with but himself.

Cody collected himself, repeating his mantra of things that kept him in the present, rescuing him from being swallowed by his past. He smiled when he realized he'd added Hannah's name to the list. A pang of guilt plagued him as he walked back to the waiting car. He'd been short with her this morning. But he was with Marci, Elena's sister, and only family member who still spoke to him. He had to stay on her good side in order to get into the private cemetery plot if he wanted to continue his ritual of self-torture.

Marci barely tolerated him as it was, so mentioning he'd have to reschedule visiting Elena to take his fake girlfriend to her tennis match wasn't an option. Their ride to and from the cemetery was silent, as always. Marci dropped him off at his house and Cody thanked her for the ride, agreeing to next month's visit.

Cody stood on the cold stone steps of his porch, watching Marci pull away. He felt the emptiness creeping back in, threatening to take hold. He looked at his uninviting front door. Home was the last place he wanted to be. He checked his watch. Hannah was probably at her tennis match. Maybe if he showed up with flowers and begged her forgiveness she'd still be willing to talk. *God knows I need some sort of distrac-*

tion, he thought. The increasing need to drink or do something to dull the pain was gnawing at him.

The heaviness of the keys in his pocket called to him. Sure, Hannah's house was only a mile away. He could walk it. He *should* walk it. But he didn't want to. It was a cold and miserable day. The heavy gray clouds promised rain. Cody grabbed the keys and jogged to the garage. He slid into the driver's seat of the Range Rover and gripped the wheel. "It's only a mile," he reminded himself.

CHAPTER
27

The rest of the ride to the tennis match went by quickly. Hannah was surprised with the ease she and Harrison conversed. He was much more down to earth than she'd assumed. And he surprisingly followed tennis, so she actually enjoyed chatting strategy with him.

When they arrived at the courts Harrison gave her a kiss on the cheek and wished her luck, saying he'd be watching from the stands. It made her nervous to have him there. The only person who'd ever come to her tennis matches was her father.

Harrison's words invaded Hannah's mind the whole time she warmed up. Especially the part about Cody being unstable. She had already witnessed Cody's mood swings and panic attacks. But despite Harrison's warning, Hannah's heart still broke for Cody. He needed help. She knew better than anyone what happened when someone tried to battle their demons alone. But she'd been through this before and as much as it killed her, Hannah had to harden herself against

Cody. She couldn't let herself be dragged down into his world of depression. She was too afraid she might not survive it.

~♡~

Luckily, the moment the match started Hannah was transported back into her comfort zone. The court was her realm and she was in control there.

The match was over quickly. Hannah won. Her opponent was a joke. Hannah strategically scheduled her matches with the easiest at the end of the season to help pad her ranking—not that she needed it. She secured the state amateur title with today's win and the purse would be a huge help with the rest of her college expenses.

She felt butterflies at her sense of accomplishment when her name was announced. Her dreams were all within reach.

She heard Harrison cheering her name from the crowd and she trotted over, unable to contain her grin.

"Way to go, Ace!" he said wrapping her in an affectionate hug.

Hannah laughed. "Thanks. But I'm all sweaty," she said wriggling out of his grasp

"I'm not complaining."

Hannah blushed. "Let me shower off and I'll meet you at the car."

~♡~

As promised, Harrison was waiting, bottle of champagne in hand.

"To your big win!"

Hannah giggled like a schoolgirl when Harrison popped the bottle and coated them in the sticky bubbles.

"Sorry," Harrison laughed wiping the champagne from her hair.

"It's okay. It's already wet."

Harrison still had his hands in her hair. "You looked hot out there."

Hannah took a big swig of champagne.

"I've always wanted to date a tennis girl. *Love* means nothing to you, right?"

Hannah rolled her eyes at his cheesy pun.

"Okay, okay. I'm sure you've heard that one before. But seriously, how do you like your ice cream? Soft serve?"

Hannah laughed. "Oh my god! I've never heard that one before!"

"Really?"

"No! Of course I've heard it. Kiss my ace, I'd hit that, Show me your backhand. I've been playing tennis since I was six. I think I've heard them all."

"Well it was worth a try," Harrison laughed. "I like you this way."

"What way?"

"Fun and smiling. You always seem so serious at school."

"I wasn't aware you paid attention to me at school," Hannah challenged, still smiling.

"Of course not. You don't give anyone a chance."

"Are you implying I'm stuck up?"

"If the tennis shoe fits . . ." Harrison smirked.

Hannah playfully nudged him. "I am *not* stuck up."

"Prove it. Let me take you out."

"We are out."

"On a date."

"What kind of date?"

"Whatever kind you'd like."

"Well . . . you do owe me for almost running me over. It's going to have to be a really nice date."

"How about dinner tomorrow to prove you're not stuck up. And . . ." Harrison reached into his pocket and pulled out a bronze skeleton key with a purple ribbon tied to it. "This is to make up for the parking lot."

Hannah's eyes grew as she reached for the key, but Harrison didn't let go.

"Come to my party with me next weekend. As my date."

"Already planning our second date?" Hannah asked, trying to play it cool although her heart was pounding. "I haven't said yes to the first one."

"You will."

CHAPTER

28

Cody arrived at Hannah's without an issue. He'd been right to drive. The rain had already started coming down. He jogged to her front door and knocked. Custard's excited barks were the only answer.

"Where's Hannah, boy? Is she still at tennis?" Cody asked Custard through the windowpane next to the door.

He wagged his tail and pawed at the glass.

"You want to come out?" Cody asked, checking the handle. *Locked.*

He felt around the top of the doorframe for a key. Then he checked under the mat. *Bingo.* Cody unlocked the door and Custard pounced on him, licking and wagging his tail in a flurry of affection.

Cody couldn't help but laugh. "You're quite the guard dog, Custard. I see you've been trained to lick intruders to death."

He put the key back and grabbed Custard's leash from its hook inside the door. He took the dog for a short walk around the house so he could do his business. The rain had turned into a fine mist that chilled Cody to the core. It was the kind of dampness that only a hot shower could rid you of. Somehow he knew showering in Hannah's house while no one was home would be frowned upon. Cody sighed. *Maybe he shouldn't have come.* He looked down at the adorable fur ball staring up at him. He was just as soaked as Cody.

Glancing around the porch Cody spotted a blanket lying over the side of an old wooden rocking chair. He picked it up and started to dry Custard's coat.

"This is our secret," he said hoping the wet dog smell wouldn't cling to the blanket. When he'd finished drying him he let Custard back inside. "There's no need for you to freeze to death." But the little dog immediately turned to see why Cody wasn't following him. "Sorry, pal. I gotta wait out here." Custard whined and pawed at the glass again. "Nope. I don't care how cute you are."

But Cody was all talk and Custard sensed his weakness. A few more seconds of whining and Cody was back at the door. "Fine, but I'm still not coming inside."

Custard happily joined Cody on the porch and settled on his lap once he sat down in one of the rocking chairs. "This better not get me in trouble. I'm already in hot water with Hannah."

Custard barked and Cody looked up to see a black limo pull into the driveway.

Shit.

—♡—

"Were you expecting company?" Harrison asked.

Hannah stiffened when she saw Cody's car in her driveway. Custard's yapping caught her attention. She barely caught a flash of his tawny fur running toward the limo before she was out the door, screaming for the world to stop.

"STOP! STOP!"

The driver slammed on the brakes but not soon enough. Hannah rounded the front of the car and crumbled to her knees. Custard lay whimpering on his side.

"No! Please, no. Custard!" Hannah sobbed as she gently buried her face in his fur. "How did you get out, baby?" she whispered.

Hannah was sure she'd locked the door. She and her father were always careful to make sure Custard couldn't get out. Since he was a puppy, chasing cars had been his vice. They'd always been extra precautious living near a busy street.

Hannah stroked his damp fur and whispered soothing words to the dog, placing his head in her lap. The driver and Harrison knelt by her side.

Cody ran toward them, pain etched across his pale features. "Shit! Hannah, I'm so sorry. He was sitting with me on the porch and—"

"You let him out?" she interrupted incredulously.

"I . . . we were waiting for you. I—"

"Why are you even here?"

Harrison interrupted, ignoring Cody completely. "Come on, Hannah. We need to get him to the vet."

She nodded, turning her back on Cody and helping Harrison lift Custard. They gently placed him on the backseat. Hannah crawled in and sat on the floor so her head was level with his. "I love you, Custard," she whispered. "You're going to be okay."

Harrison got in, with Cody on his heels. "I think you'd better sit this one out," he warned Cody.

"I want to help."

"You've done plenty."

"Hannah," Cody pleaded, "I'm so sorry. Please let me come with you."

"Go home, Cody!"

Harrison pulled the door shut and they sped away, leaving Cody alone in the rain.

CHAPTER
29

Cody drove home in stunned silence. The windshield wipers rhythmically whispering all the wrong he'd done. His house was cold and empty. His thoughts echoed around him as he grabbed a bottle of Jack on his way to his room. He kept the lights off. He didn't want to see himself. Cody turned on his music as loud as he could to drown out his thoughts and then uncapped the Jack, swallowing the liquid—praying it would drown years of regret.

Cody looked around, uncertain of the time or what woke him, but his room was bathed in darkness and silence. He jumped when his bedside lamp flicked on and the world slowly came into focus. Hannah stood feet from him, her eyes puffy and hair undone.

Everything came flashing back.

Cody slid from the bed and crashed to his knees, throwing his arms around Hannah's waist. "I'm so sorry. Hannah, I never meant to hurt him."

She shoved him off with disgust. "Are you drunk?"

"I . . . yes," he admitted shamefully.

He couldn't lie to her. Not after what he'd done. He looked up at her and could see hate simmering in her blue eyes. His heart cracked wide open. He knew it wouldn't matter what he said to Hannah. She'd given up on him, just like everyone else. And he couldn't even blame her.

"Why were you at my house, Cody?"

"I wanted to talk . . . and apologize for this morning."

"So you thought breaking in and letting my dog loose was the best plan?"

"No. He—"

"He's going to be fine, by the way. Thanks for asking."

"He is?" Cody stood up clinging to a glimmer of hope.

"He has a few broken bones but there's no internal bleeding so the vet said he should be fine."

"That's such good news."

"Yes, Custard will be fine, but we're not." Hannah pulled the skeleton key Cody had given her from her purse and placed it on the bedside table. "We're done, Cody."

"But what about the party?"

"I'll be going with Harrison. He gave me my own key. I don't need yours. I don't need anything from you anymore."

"He gave you a key?"

"Yes. So you don't have to pretend to be my boyfriend any longer."

"Hannah, don't go to that party with him. You can't trust him."

"Funny. He said the same thing about you."

"Hannah—"

"Look, I just came here to return your key and tell you I'm done with our arrangement. Please leave me alone, Cody." Hannah stormed out of Cody's room, leaving her fragrance behind to eat a hole through his heart.

What did he expect? He was a fuck up and everyone knew it. And now, so did Hannah.

Cody sat on the edge of his bed before sliding to the floor. His hand sought out the bottle of Jack. It was almost empty. A problem he planned to remedy. He knew there'd be no solution at the bottom of it. But it seemed the lesser of all the evils he could think of at the moment.

CHAPTER

30

Hannah deferred her dinner plans with Harrison. Truthfully, she'd lost her taste for her twisted game. After what happened to her dog, she wasn't sure she cared about conquering the Goldens. She didn't want to involve herself any further in their messed up world.

She and her father brought Custard home from the vet Monday morning. Hannah stayed home from school to help care for him, convincing her father that with only a few days of school left, she wasn't missing anything important.

Harrison was surprisingly sweet through the whole ordeal. He brought over flowers and a huge, fluffy pet bed for Custard. He even offered to cook dinner for her and her father rather than taking her out. Hannah graciously declined and promised to go out to dinner with him later when things calmed down. Her father had been near hysterics after hearing about the events that led to Custard's accident. He wasn't too keen on having Harrison around.

When Hannah inevitably returned to Stanton on Tuesday, the campus seemed like an alien planet. Harrison greeted her in the parking lot with something hot, delicious and caffeinated from Starbucks. He put his arm around her and walked her to class. Savannah and her minions gave her hugs between classes and feigned concern for her 'poor, sweet' dog—*whom they'd never met.* They made sure Hannah knew they were there for her and that they weren't shocked Cody was to blame.

At lunch, Harrison was waiting to whisk Hannah up to the Golden Gate, where more people she didn't know suffocated her with fake concern. She couldn't believe she'd ever envied the Goldens. Yes they swam in the beautiful gene pool and had limitless trust funds, but now that she was on the inside she could see how hollow they were. The only one who seemed to have any substance was Harrison. He was actually really sweet. He made a point to walk her to and from class, he bought her lunch and rescued her from conversations that turned to Cody bashing—which was often. Luckily Cody hadn't been at school all week, so Hannah was spared from avoiding him.

On Thursday her luck ran out.

Cody walked under the Golden Gate, his hands stuffed in his pockets, head down. But Savannah and the rest of the Goldens weren't going to let him go by unscathed.

"The dog slayer lives," Savannah called loudly. "See, Hannah. I told you not to worry. You can't kill a cockroach."

Cody stopped walking and slowly turned around.

Keep walking, Hannah willed. She didn't think she could stomach a full on Golden assault. And from the looks of Cody, neither could he. He was unshaven and dark circles clung under his eyes.

Cody glared up at them, his pained eyes stinging Hannah. "You're not one of them, Hannah. You never will be."

"And neither are you," Blakely scathed.

"Don't try to drag Hannah down just because you fucked up your life and now you're nothing," Savannah hissed.

"Let's leave Hannah out of this," Harrison said, possessively pulling her closer to him.

Cody bristled at the intimate gesture before shaking his head. "You're better than them, Hannah," he called before skulking away from the jeering crowd.

Finally the school day was over. Seeing Cody looking so disheveled turned Hannah's stomach sour and she'd been counting the minutes until she could flee campus. She just wanted to go home to snuggle Custard and shut the world out. She hated that she had a hand in causing Cody more pain. He was already suffering. She knew deep down he hadn't meant to hurt Custard. She'd seen the way Cody was with him, playing and roughhousing—it was love at first sight with them. And if she was honest, seeing Cody babble baby talk to her dog had unglued something in her heart. It also made her doubt Harrison's story of Cody's violent past.

Hannah knew she'd been too harsh with Cody. She'd been caught up in the trauma of the accident and then her days were filled with his ex-friends, more than happy to stoke her resentment. But it wasn't an excuse. She needed to apologize. Hannah massaged her temples as she walked to her car. *Cody was right.* He warned her that she couldn't get too close to the Goldens without being poisoned by them.

She was just getting to her car when Harrison called her name. She turned to see him jogging toward her. His face was glowing with a smarmy smile that her gut refused to trust. Suddenly she wanted out. This game had been a terrible idea.

"Hey, beautiful. You weren't leaving without saying goodbye, were you?" he asked displaying his best pout. "I thought we could finally have our date tonight?"

"Oh, I don't think I'm up for it tonight."

Harrison looked genuinely crestfallen. "I'm sorry about today . . . with Cody."

Hannah was momentarily stunned by his perception. But she was tired of the dread that had been following her around the last few days. She needed to end this. Cut ties and put her life back to normal. Plain, boring—vanilla.

"Harrison, I really appreciate how kind you've been, but I don't think this is going to work out."

"What? Why not?

"We're from two different worlds."

"Different worlds?"

"Come on. You can't tell me you don't see it. You live in another stratosphere."

"I get it," he sneered. "You think I live a charmed life, just like everyone else."

"I didn't say that—"

"Well let me tell you, Hannah. It's not all been a fairytale. I'm just a guy and I thought we had a connection. I thought I'd finally found someone who didn't see me as a trophy or a prick. But I guess I was wrong."

"No, Harrison. It's not like that. I just . . ."

"You just what?" he growled.

"I have a hard time believing someone like you could actually like someone like me."

Harrison's face softened and he took Hannah's hands. "I don't know how I never saw you until now, but I can't let you go."

His blue eyes bore into Hannah's and she wavered.

"Listen, you've been under a lot of stress. You deserve a break. We both do. Let's get away from all of this and see if there's really something between us. Without tennis and vets and Stanton. Let me take you to dinner."

"Just dinner?"

"Yes. Just dinner."

Hannah's heart fought her gut. She looked at the ground to hide her internal struggle.

Harrison gently tugged her chin so he could see her face. "Look, I don't know what this is, but I'm willing to explore if you are. Worse case you get a nice dinner." His perfect teeth blazed a practiced smile. "I promise to take you somewhere great."

He was handsome and charming and he was directing all of it at her. Hannah's inner goddess was doing backflips and promised to kill her if she denied herself a dinner date with a real life prince charming. "Fine."

"Great! I'll pick you up at six."

CHAPTER

31

At six o'clock sharp Harrison pulled up outside Hannah's house in a white Mercedes G-class. *At least it wasn't the limo*, Hannah thought gratefully as she kissed her father's cheek and ran out the door before he could badger her with more questions. It'd been hard enough to convince him to let her go to dinner with Harrison. But it appeared he even started to win her father over after all the kindness Harrison showed them after Custard's accident.

Harrison opened the car door for Hannah and she hopped in.

"How many cars do you have?" she asked studying the roomy interior enviously as he pulled away.

He laughed. "They're sort of my father's obsession. We've got quite a collection if you'd like to see it some time?"

"Maybe. We'll see how tonight goes."

He gave her another dazzling smile. "I think you'll be impressed."

"Someone's feeling confident."

"Well, I did pull out all the stops."

"What does that mean?"

"You'll see."

"We *are* going to dinner, right? I haven't eaten since lunch and I'm starving."

Harrison laughed. "Good. You're probably better off on an empty stomach. It can be a bit of a bumpy ride."

"What?"

As Hannah asked the question, they turned off the road and approached a gate with a call box. Harrison rolled down the window and punched in a code and the gate began to open. They rumbled up the drive to the top of a hill covered in lights and industrial looking sheds. It was a private airport!

"We're having dinner in Boston, right?" Hannah asked trying to conceal her mild panic.

"Yes. Sort of. Come on."

Harrison parked and led Hannah around one of the large white buildings. A tiny white helicopter glowed under a pool of light and Harrison waved to the two men standing beside it.

"Oh my god! Is that how we're getting to dinner?"

"You're the one who said I live in a different stratosphere." He winked. "Just keeping the fairytale alive."

꙳

The ride to dinner was amazing. Seeing Boston at sunset from the sky was one of the most beautiful sights Hannah had ever experienced. As promised, it'd been a bumpy ride and she clung to Harrison unable to contain her squeals when her stomach dropped with the turbulence. He'd surprised her by laughing and hollering right along with her, squeezing her hand and pointing out some of his favorite landmarks.

The helicopter ride reminded Hannah of the terrifying rides at the fair. The ones she could never bring herself to brave as she sat enviously watching couples cling to each other with an equal balance of fear and love as their world spun out of control. She was finally seeing that's what relationships were—finding someone to hold onto in the chaos and hoping they wouldn't let go.

Their awe-inspiring flight ended with Hannah and Harrison landing safely on a giant yacht. Hannah recognized it instantly. It was a fixture at Boston Harbor, dwarfing all the other vessels. At 126 meters it was hard to miss. Hannah shaded her eyes reading the vessel's name. *Coalescence*. She'd grown up seeing it at the harbor; always assuming it was some sort of ritzy tourist cruise line.

"We're having dinner here?" she asked bewildered as Harrison took her hand and helped her out of the helicopter.

"Yes. And don't worry, we're still technically in Boston. We won't leave the harbor."

He led her to the empty cream and gray lounge. A cozy table for two had been set up next to the massive windows, giving them a gorgeous view of the glowing lights of the harbor. A loud blast from the ship's horn startled Hannah and she noticed the lights of the city began to move as they drifted away.

She gazed around at the empty lounge. "Are we going out by ourselves?"

"The crew's on board. But yes, no other passengers." Harrison took note of her shock. "Unless you're uncomfortable being alone with me."

"No, it's not that. It's just . . . you didn't have to rent out the whole boat just for us."

He smirked and looked down, cheeks reddening. "I didn't rent it. It's my father's yacht."

"Oh. Coalescence! I get it now. I guess I should have put that together."

Harrison grinned and signaled for the waiter who appeared out of nowhere. He poured them both mineral water and brought menus.

Hannah was at a loss for words. She knew the Cohl's were wealthy, but this was beyond comprehension. They were having dinner on their own floating city. *How could she have anything in common with someone who could arrange this on a whim?*

"This was too much wasn't it?" Harrison asked after ordering for them both.

"No. I . . ." she didn't know what to say. Dinner on a private yacht wasn't something Hannah was prepared for.

"Shit. He was right."

"Who?"

"Don't get mad."

"About what?"

"I asked Cody about you."

"What?"

"He and I aren't exactly friends but I wanted to make sure you guys were over before I asked you out. He assured me there was nothing between you."

A pang of hurt pierced Hannah's heart. *Nothing,* that's what she was to Cody.

"I asked for dinner tips and he said to play it cool, that you wouldn't like anything fancy."

"What does Cody know? I can be fancy!" she blurted out.

Harrison held up his hands in surrender. "I'm sorry. I shouldn't have brought it up. It's just I don't want to start out on the wrong foot, keeping things from you."

Guilt dried Hannah's throat and she took a gulp of her Chardonnay. It didn't help. The oaky flavor tasted like tree bark sliding down her throat. "What else did Cody have to say about me?"

"Nothing. Honestly, let's leave Cody out of this. I think we're doing pretty well on our own."

They made small talk through dinner, but Hannah's mind kept snapping back to Cody. She was impressed he hadn't told Harrison about her ulterior motives. But she would have to talk to Cody and swear him to secrecy, because she was starting to actually like Harrison. And she didn't want Cody to ruin things. Plus, a tiny part of Hannah hated that Cody had been discussing her, like an old coat he was passing off. Calling her ordinary, not something to dress up and take out.

After dinner Harrison took Hannah on a tour of the yacht. She was amazed at the extravagance of it all.

"A movie theater? Seriously? Who needs a movie theater when you have views of the ocean?" she asked as they toured the private theater room.

"And you haven't even seen the best view! Come on," Harrison took Hannah by the hand and pulled her excitedly behind him. He was like a kid at Christmas on the yacht. It was obvious that he was passionate about the water as he spouted off nautical words that meant nothing to Hannah, and filled her head with stories of the exotic places he'd sailed to.

Perhaps it was the intoxicating luxury of the yacht or maybe the wine, but Hannah couldn't help herself, she let her imagination run wild and she trotted after Harrison. *Why couldn't this fantasy world be true? Maybe he really did want to spend time with her. Maybe they'd even sail to adventurous places together.*

They burst into a two-story room and Hannah gasped at its unfathomable beauty. Floor to ceiling windows framed the posh white bedroom. A plush king sized bed rested in the center of the clear second floor balcony. Harrison pulled Hannah up the clear spiral staircase and plopped down on the bed.

He patted the spot next to him. "*This is where you get the best views.*"

Hannah sat down on the edge of the bed and sighed taking in the rainbow of city lights reflecting off the water. "It's gorgeous."

Harrison flopped onto his back and looked up at Hannah. "You're gorgeous."

She blushed as he reached up to stroke a tendril of her blonde hair.

"You surprise me, Hannah. Not many girls do."

"I can say the same about you."

Harrison rose to his elbows. Their faces invaded each other's space. Hannah could feel the warmth of his breath on her lips. Their eyes met for a moment, just before their lips did. Hannah let Harrison take control, allowing herself to be lost in a momentary flurry of passion. Lips, tongues, hands—all fumbling in a hungry desire for each other. Waves of heat radiated through her as Harrison tore off his shirt and pulled hers away too. He kissed her again, pressing her into the bed, his body firm against hers. He tugged down her bra straps. The intimacy made her freeze. *She wasn't ready.* It was all going too fast.

"Wait," she begged, breathlessly.

"What's wrong," Harrison panted.

"Don't you want to talk more?"

"I like it better when we don't talk," he purred trailing kisses down her neck to her breasts.

She pushed him away and vaulted off the bed, pacing near the stairs like a caged animal.

"Hannah?"

"I'm sorry. I thought I was ready for this, but I'm not," she choked out. Her face reddened with embarrassment.

Harrison climbed off the bed and padded over, her shirt in hand. "Here," he said softly tugging it back over her head. "We don't have to do anything you don't want to, Hannah. I'm just happy to spend time with you."

"Really?" she asked looking up timidly, her head poking through the neck of her clingy white sweater.

Harrison grinned and kissed her messy hair. "Really." He put on his shirt and took Hannah's hand. "Come on. We're heading back to port and you have to see the stars from the observation deck."

CHAPTER
32

Hannah and Harrison snuggled on the observation deck under a thick white blanket while they watched the stars twinkle over Boston. Hannah's nose was frozen and her cheeks rosy from the chilled salt air, but she found herself reluctant to leave the warmth she'd found nestled next to Harrison when they arrived back at the marina.

He'd surprised Hannah by being a complete gentleman, saving the night by not letting her embarrassing inexperience ruin his mood. She expected him to be pissed that she didn't put out after his elaborate date, but he seemed to genuinely be having a good time in her company, content with kissing under the stars.

When their date was over and Harrison walked Hannah to her door he asked when they could do it again.

"So I didn't totally screw this up?" she asked.

"Hannah, what do I have to say to get you to trust me?"

She sighed. "I'm sorry. It's just you're too good to be true."

"I could say the same thing about you." He kissed her lightly. "Say we can do this again?" he whispered.

"Okay, okay. I think I can suffer another evening on your yacht if I must."

Harrison picked her up in a delighted embrace and she giggled. "That-a-girl," he joked kissing her again. "By the way, I won't be at school tomorrow. I have some last minute arrangements to attend to before the party on Saturday."

"What kind of arrangements?"

"You must allow me to keep some of my mystique," he joked, bowing and backing away toward his car.

Hannah couldn't help but swoon. *She was smitten! How did this happen?*

"You *are* still my date to the ball, right?" he called back to her.

"If you'll still have me."

He grinned wickedly. "I wouldn't have anyone else."

"Then I'll meet you there."

"Don't be late, Cinderella. I'll be the one in the mask."

Hannah waved after Harrison as he drove away, then quickly let herself inside. Leaning against the front door for support, she closed her eyes and sighed, reliving the delicious moments of her date.

"Have fun?"

Hannah's eyes flew open. Her father was peering at her over his reading glasses. He was camouflaged among the books and blankets covering his lap.

"Were you waiting up for me?"

"You bet I was."

Hannah rolled her eyes. "Yes, I had fun. Harrison was a gentleman."

"Where'd you go?"

"Dinner," she paused not wanting to lie to her father. "On the water."

"I'm glad you had fun. Now go to your room and never date again."

"Daaaad," she groaned, marching over to give him a kiss on the head. "I have to grow up sometime."

"I know," he grumbled. "That's what I'm afraid of."

Hannah smiled and made her way upstairs wanting to avoid a fatherly lecture. Her father was rarely doting, but she still hated the feeling of suffocation it brought. She and her father normally had a functional relationship. They worked more like colleagues than parent and child—tackling tasks like groceries, household chores and appointments like efficient business partners. But boys were a new division and it was apparent her father wasn't on board with that venture. The only other time he'd been this neurotic was when Hannah learned to drive.

Hannah showered quickly and flopped into bed. It was late, but her body hummed with excitement. Every time she closed her eyes she pictured Harrison's flawless body pressed into hers. His delicious lips igniting fire everywhere they touched.

How had she let such a perfect moment pass her by?

Hannah cursed herself for being a virgin. She'd wasted so much time focusing on academics and accolades that she'd missed out on the adventure and affection of adolescence. Tonight was proof of that. She'd been right to want to explore her freedom in the time she had left. If tonight was any indication, Harrison was the right guy to fill in what her education was lacking. And the thought of it was exhilarating.

Her phone buzzed and she picked it up.

ARE YOU STILL AWAKE? – HARRISON

YES – HANNAH

I CAN'T STOP THINKING ABOUT YOU – HARRISON

Hannah rolled over, kicked her feet excitedly and screamed into her pillow as butterflies rioted in her stomach.

So this is what all the fuss is about?

Hannah's heart sored and her lungs felt crushed. In just one date she'd fallen for Harrison Cohl—and she'd never felt better.

Hannah rolled back over and grabbed her phone, texting a smiley face.

X – HARRISON

X – HANNAH

Hannah fell asleep with the phone clutched to her chest, her inner goddess glowing enough to light the entire city of Boston.

CHAPTER

33

"So the party's tomorrow night!" Savannah purred. "What are you going to wear, Hannah?"

With Harrison gone, arranging the final details for his party, Hannah found herself sitting on the Golden Gate with Savannah, Madison and Blakely. She ate her PB&J while they sipped their juices. They were cleansing. Apparently they fasted for 36 hours before any posh event and were appalled that Hannah didn't know proper starvation etiquette.

"I'm not sure. I haven't had time to really shop. I'm sure I'll find something in my closet though."

All three girls put their green sludge down staring at Hannah like she'd said she was planning on showing up naked.

"You can't just wear anything to a Cohl ball!" Madison whispered.

"It's a masquerade. You *do* know that, right?" Blakely sneered.

"Of course."

Savannah piped up. "I have an idea! Why don't you all come to my place tonight and we'll try on our dresses for the party. Hannah, you can shop in my closet," she offered sweetly. "I have plenty of masks from prior years."

"I'll supply the cocktails!" Blakely added.

"Cocktail party!" they sang in unison, clinking their juice glasses together, leaving Hannah to feel like the outsider she was.

Hannah gawked as she pulled up to Savannah's house after school. She would never get used to this kind of ostentatiousness. Savannah's home was almost a carbon copy of Cody's McMansion and Hannah found herself wondering if they were doled out once you reached a certain tax bracket.

At least the interior of Savannah's home was more inviting than Cody's. Colorful art in gaudy gold frames hung on the walls, bright floral arrangements graced nearly every surface and blaring music danced toward Hannah from somewhere upstairs. A staff member led her to Savannah's room, where she, Blakely and Madison were lounging around in their expensive underwear sipping champagne among the carnage of lavish dresses. It seems the contents of Savannah's closet had exploded, and exhausted by the idea of trying on anything else the girls turned to gossip and booze.

"Hannah! I'm so glad you made it," Savannah shouted over the house music passing a glass of bubbly her way. "We'd begun to think you'd stood us up," she pouted.

"No, I just had to go home first. Clear it with my dad. You know how it is."

All three girls cocked their heads, perplexed by Hannah's comment. They reminded Hannah of cats watching a fish tank. Apparently the concept of parental control wasn't something they worried about.

Hannah told her dad she'd been invited to Savannah's to work on plans for the commencement ceremony. She hated lying to him and rather than trying to explain her father's complex parenting style to the girls, Hannah decided to drown her guilt with a sip of champagne.

It was divine! Hannah actually sighed out loud.

"I know, right?" Blakely grinned, topping off her own glass.

"So, what do you want to wear to the ball?" Madison asked, pointing to the piles of dresses lying about Savannah's overly magenta room.

"I don't know. Which ones are you girls wearing?" Hannah asked taking another swig of liquid courage in anticipation of trying on dresses in front of the Goldens.

They were already raking their eyes over her in a predatorily way. She suddenly found herself longing for Cody's fashion advice. He'd at least been constructive with his criticism. Somehow she knew these girls wouldn't hold back.

"Oh, we ordered our dresses from our favorite designers months ago," Savannah replied with a haughty laugh. She grabbed a garment bag from her closet.

"Yeah, like we'd wear off the rack," Blakely scoffed.

The girls each pulled long slinky gowns from the garment bag. Savannah's was unsurprisingly magenta, Blakely's a shimmering jade and Madison's, classic black.

"We pulled out a couple options for you, but feel free to have at it," Savannah said motioning to her closet.

Hannah gulped. "Okay. Thanks." She entered the cavernous closet and tried not to drool.

"So," Madison pried. "You never told us how your date with Harrison was last night."

"Oh, it was great," Hannah replied a little too eagerly.

The girls giggled and Hannah popped her head out of the closet. "What?"

"Oh nothing, it's just we've heard that swoon before," Savannah laughed. "A Cohl has charmed the panties off another one."

"No it wasn't like that," Hannah defended.

"Sure . . ."

"No really, we just had dinner."

"Where'd he take you?" Blakely asked trying on a pair of silver stilettos.

"His yacht."

"His *yacht!*" Madison exclaimed. Savannah elbowed her for the outburst.

"Okay you can give up the innocent act," Blakely scathed. "If you've been on his yacht, you're a Cohl-hole."

"A what?"

Savannah laughed. "That's what we call the girls that have slept with one of the Cohl boys."

"Yeah and you have that look," Blakely accused.

"Takes one to know one," Savannah teased.

"Omigod! I haven't slept with anyone!" Hannah blurted.

The room stopped, all eyes targeted her.

"Are you a virgin?" Madison whispered.

Shit! Hannah downed the rest of her champagne, stalling. There was no use lying now. It was probably written all over her face anyway. Maybe she could get some advice out of it. But it was going to take a lot more champagne. Hannah held out her empty glass and nodded, biting her bottom lip.

The girls erupted with shrieks and laughter. But to Hannah's surprise they didn't seem to be laughing at her. They actually seemed delighted.

"Well then, we're going to help you make tomorrow a night you won't forget!" Savannah grinned, handing Hannah another glass of bubbly. "Come on girls! Forget the dress. She'll be focused on getting it off anyway."

"Or just getting off!" Madison giggled.

For the next hour they refilled Hannah's glass while filling her head with the do's and don'ts of first time sex. And they weren't bashful. Savannah pulled up videos on YouTube and Blakely even gave animated demonstrations. Hannah felt like she'd been through sex boot camp by the time they were done. They really seemed to take their mission, which they'd dubbed, 'Banana for Hannah', seriously.

She should have come here and left Cody out of it.

"What's this about Cody?" Savannah asked.

Oh shit! Had she said that out loud?

Hannah's head was swimming. She set down her empty champagne glass.

"Cody?"

"You just said you should have left Cody out of it."

"I did?"

"Yes," Savannah pressed. "What's the deal with you two anyway? I thought you were done."

"Yeah and now we know you weren't using him for sex," Madison chimed in.

"Shame," Blakely added indifferently. "He *is* a loser, but it would've been nice to use him to pop your cherry so you don't ruin Harrison's Italian sheets."

"Cody and I are done," Hannah said hoping to end the

subject. "I mean there really wasn't anything to begin with."

"Are you sure?" Savannah asked, her icy stare pinning Hannah.

"Yes."

"Good. Cause I'd hate to see Harrison get hurt if you weren't serious about him. He's one of our dearest friends, you know?"

Hannah gulped down her fear and nodded.

Savannah sighed. "I told you it was just gossip, girls," she mused turning to admire her reflection.

"What's gossip?" Hannah asked.

"Oh you know Cody. He's just running his mouth about the two of you."

Hannah's blood went cold. "What's he saying?"

"I wouldn't worry about it. I'm sure no one will take anything he says seriously."

"God, you're *so* lucky Harrison almost hit you with his car," Madison added, smiling sweetly. "Otherwise you would still be slumming it in wasteville with Cody."

"Yeah," Hannah whispered, her vision tunneling. *How much champagne had she drank?*

Blakely snorted. "Too bad Harrison didn't hit Cody with his car. Then we could forget about him already."

"I think I should go home," Hannah blurted out.

"Blakely, you've upset her! You always take things too far," Savannah scolded. She put her arm around Hannah and steered her into the en suite bathroom. "I'm sorry about that, sweetie." She put her hands on her hips. "You look a little flushed. You're not a virgin to alcohol too, are you?"

"No. I just feel a little lightheaded."

"Good, because I'd hate for you puke on my bathroom

floor." Savannah giggled. "How about I give you a ride home. I don't want to take any chances of you getting a DUI and missing your big night tomorrow."

"My car—"

"I'll have one of our staff return it tomorrow."

"Oh, I don't want to impose."

"Nonsense. Come on, the girls can entertain themselves for a while."

When they walked back into the bedroom, Madison and Blakely were trading stories about the legendary conquests of the Cohl boys. Their shrill voices did nothing to ease Hannah's dizziness. She wanted to go home and lay down. All this talk about tomorrow was overwhelming her.

"I'm taking Hannah home," Savannah announced to the room, scooping up the silver gown they'd picked out for her.

"Bye," the girls purred in unison.

⁓

As soon as Savannah pulled out of her driveway she took Hannah's hand and whispered hurriedly. "Listen, I didn't want to say too much in front of the girls—they can be gossipy—but Cody has been spreading vicious rumors about you."

"What? Why?"

Savannah shrugged. "I really think it might be in your best interest to nip it in the bud before word gets around at the ball."

"But how? The ball is tomorrow," Hannah moaned.

"Shit, you're right. Oh, Hannah, I'd just hate for Harrison to find out. You two are so cute together and he could really use a sweet girl like you."

Hannah closed her eyes feeling angry and tired. Just when things were starting to line up for her, Cody was going to ruin it all. This was her payback for blackmailing him. She rubbed her eyes to get some clarity and Savannah mistook it for crying.

"My god, don't cry! We can solve this."

"How?"

"What if I take you over there right now?"

"To Cody's? Now?" Hannah glanced at the dash display. "It's 10 o'clock."

"So, it's Friday night. Do you want to fix this, or not?"

"What do I even say to him?"

"I don't know. Just tell him to leave you alone and stop spreading rumors. Cody and Harrison have a rocky history. You don't want to let this catch fire."

"It would help if I knew what kind of rumors he was spreading."

"He said he slept with you, alright!"

"What?"

"I didn't want to have to say it because I knew you'd be upset."

"But I didn't sleep with him!"

"I know. I believe you. It's Harrison we have to worry about."

After an awkward silence Savannah drawled out a sentence. "You know . . . it really is a shame you haven't slept with Cody."

"Why?"

"Well, I think Blakely was right. It'd take the edge off things with Harrison and then Cody's rumors wouldn't be rumors. It might shut him up."

Hannah glared at Savannah. "I'm not sleeping with Cody to shut him up."

"It was just a thought!"

Savannah pulled into Cody's driveway. The house was dark as usual.

"So you go do your thing. I'm gonna head downtown. The girls just texted. They decided to go to Bar None. Our favorite college band is playing. They are drool-worthy! Just text me when you're done and I'll come back and get you so you can come party with us."

"Thanks for all your help tonight, Savannah. I really appreciate it. But I'm all partied out. I only live a few blocks away. I can walk it."

"Are you sure?"

"Yeah, this won't be pleasant. I'm sure the fresh air will do me good."

"Okay, well text me later. I wanna know how it went." Savannah blew her a kiss. "Oh and I'll send your dress over with your car in the morning. See you tomorrow."

Hannah watched Savannah's sporty silver Mercedes zip out of Cody's driveway. She turned toward the door took a deep breath before pushing the buzzer. It took her three tries to hit it. All of this stress must have been making her vision hazy. She needed to get this over. *Just like ripping off a Band-Aid.* She would make him a new deal. Keep his mouth shut or the school gets his test scores.

♡

Savannah was barely out of the driveway before she tapped out a text message.

WORRIED ABOUT HANNAH. SHE'S DRUNK –
SAVANNAH

She hit send, and grinned like a Cheshire cat when she
saw an immediate response pop up.

WHERE – HARRISON

"This is going to be fun," she said to herself.

CODY'S – SAVANNAH

WTF!!! – HARRISON

CHAPTER
34

Cody sat on his floor, bottle of Jack between his legs, while he attacked his game console. He was blaring the volume through his headphones and taking out his frustrations the best way he knew how. *Okay, almost the best way.* He was still relying heavily on his old friend, Jack. He was a fair bit hammered, but it was Friday night, and at least he was channeling his anger at the war game currently raging on his plasma screen.

That's why when he felt a hand on his shoulder he nearly pissed himself. Cody jumped to his feet spilling half the bottle of Jack on the carpet. He righted it and whirled around trying to get his eyes to focus in the darkness. He must have been more snockered than he thought, because it appeared that Hannah was standing in his room, looking royally pissed off.

"Hannah?" he asked not believing his eyes.

"How dare you?" she yelled, sloppily shoving him.

"Are you drunk?" Cody asked taking in her wobbly appearance.

"Oh, you're one to talk!" she shouted moving to push him again.

She lost her footing and collided with Cody. It was more force than he was anticipating and they both toppled onto his bed.

"Let go of me!" she howled.

Cody held his arms up in surrender but couldn't help from bursting into laughter. "Honestly, what's wrong with you? You're the one that's on top of me."

"You need to take some responsibility too, Cody," Hannah slurred, still not moving from her spot atop him.

"What are you talking about?"

"I always have to clean up your messes and I'm over it. I'm over you! I've told you that before. Now please leave me alone!"

"Did you seriously come over her to tackle me and tell me to leave you alone?" he asked, his temper flaring. "Because you've made that clear, Hannah. You don't need to kick me while I'm down."

"That's not what I'm doing."

"Then what *are* you doing?" Cody growled, fighting his body's reflex to hers. Her legs straddled his hips and her hands pressed into his chest for support. He couldn't stop staring at her eyes. They were wild with . . . he didn't know what. *Was it lust? Or did he just want it to be?*

She leaned closer and her long hair brushed his cheek. "I don't know."

Cody brushed her hair away, following the strand to her cheek. Her face was hot and she let out the tiniest gasp when he touched her. It was his undoing. His restraint unraveled and he pulled her lips to his, meeting in a furious crash of passion. He craved her in a way he didn't understand. She was the only thing that could drown out the hurt and he couldn't get enough. He wanted to wrap his body in hers until there was nothing left between them. He'd known it the moment he saw her in the fitting room—she bared her soul to him and that's what terrified him. Hannah was pure and perfect, and he knew he would ruin her.

<hr />

Hannah stripped her clothes away feverishly, while Cody fisted her hair, keeping her close to him with trembling hands. His kiss devoured her, setting something loose deep inside her.

She wanted this.

Not like this.

She needed this.

Not like this!

Her mind and body warred, but her invading hormones won out. Cody groaned into her mouth when she slipped her hand under the waistband of his thin lounge pants. Her power over him was intoxicating. The more she touched the more he needed, whispering her name like a secret prayer.

She slid down his rigid torso, begging her hands to memorize his perfection. Before she could reach her target Cody hauled her back to him, his eyes wide and pleading. "Hannah." He said her name sternly. "I don't think we should do this right now."

"Are you serious?"

"Are you?"

"Yes. I want to do this." She pushed passed his guard and kissed him again, luring him in with the coaxing rhythm of her hips and lips.

"Shit, Hannah." He flipped her onto her back pinning her beneath him. "I want to do this so badly. You have *no* idea," he groaned. "But this isn't right. You're drunk and you . . . you hate me. This isn't how it should be."

"I'm not drunk. I had a few glasses of champagne."

"You've had more than a few glasses to dull hate to lust."

"I don't hate you, Cody."

"I saw the way you looked at me after the vet. You hate me."

"I may not always understand you, but I don't hate you. Believe me, I've tried and I should. But—."

"What do you mean you should?"

"Don't play dumb. I know you've been talking about me."

"To who?"

"Does it really matter?"

"Yes!"

"Harrison and others."

"Why the hell would I talk to Harrison?"

Hannah shook her head. "Do you really think I'm not fancy?"

"What?"

"That's what you told him, didn't you? That I'm just plain and casual. That I couldn't possibly enjoy being spoiled?"

"Hannah! I never said that. I've never said anything about you. To anyone!"

"I find that hard to believe when Savannah told me just tonight she heard you saying we slept together!"

Cody pushed himself off the bed angrily. He paced, running his hands through his hair. He turned back to Hannah, his temper barely caged. "They're lying to you, Hannah. This is what they do. They fuck with people for fun. They get off on it. I would never say that about you."

"Why not, it's just sex right? It's not a big deal."

"That's just it, Hannah. It is a big deal! It's supposed to be a big deal!"

"Not for you! I'm sure you've done it a thousand times."

"I haven't!" Cody shouted grabbing Hannah's arms roughly as if trying to force understanding into her.

Hannah's heart pounded as she tried to wrap her fuzzy mind around what Cody was saying. "Haven't . . . as in ever?" She stared at the blazing truth in his eyes, barely aware she was only wearing her bra and panties. Her efforts remained on staying upright and making sense of what Cody was saying. She cursed herself for drinking so much champagne. Everything was swaying.

"But I thought . . . I thought Elena was pregnant . . ." she stammered. "Cody, what are you saying?"

"Elena was pregnant. But it wasn't mine. That's what our fight was about the night . . ." He couldn't finish his sentence. His eyes darted around the room looking for something solid to cling to. When they settled on the bottle of Jack he moved toward it, knocking back a huge gulp.

"How do you know it wasn't yours?"

Cody laughed and sank down onto the bed. "Because I never had sex with Elena. I've never had sex with anyone. She was cheating on me because I wanted to wait."

"What?"

He took another long swig and shook his head. "That's right, Casanova Cody is a fraud."

"Do you know who . . . who the father is . . . was?"

Cody grimaced and collapsed back onto the bed in frustration.

Hannah sighed thinking Cody was done with the subject until she heard his voice, barely above a whisper. "I've got a pretty good idea."

She leaned back on the bed, bringing her face close to his. "Have you ever told anyone?"

He continued to stare at the ceiling. "I can't prove anything. And who's going to believe me. I'm just another fuck up."

"But it's the truth."

"It wouldn't matter."

"It would matter to me," she said softly, slipping her hand into his. He pulled away and sat up again. Grabbing for the Jack on the nightstand. Hannah sat up too. She watched him take another long drink from the near empty bottle, trying to grasp these revelations. "Cody, it might matter to a lot of people. Like Elena's family. Your family."

He snorted. "Thanks but you don't have to say that."

"I'm not just saying it. You're being blamed for more than driving drunk. Everyone thinks you got her pregnant and then killed her to get rid of the problem. Don't you want to set the record straight?"

Cody laughed a bit hysterically, prompting Hannah to take the bottle from him. "You're gonna need it," he snorted. "You ready for the best part? I wasn't even the one driving. I'd been drinking but I still knew enough not to get behind the wheel. But Elena . . . she was wasted and screaming about the pregnancy and her life being ruined and saying everything was my fault. She just wanted to get away from it all." He laughed sadly. "I don't blame her. She was scared and lashing out. I was just the closest target. We hurt the ones we love the most, right?"

A sobering thought dragged its icy claws down Hannah's back.

No. It couldn't be true. No one would suffer as he had if . . . if . . .

"Cody, if you weren't driving that night . . ."

"It was Elena. She was hysterical. I'd driven us to the party and she wanted to leave. I told her I couldn't drive and she just got in my car and started to drive off. I couldn't let her go like that. Not by herself. I jumped in and begged her to calm down and talk it out, but she wouldn't hear me. She'd just worked herself up, ya know?" Cody's shaking hands scrubbed at his face, wrestling with the crippling truth. "I loved her. I just wanted to be there for her."

Hannah's hands shook as she covered her mouth, fighting the taste of bile at her realization. "Elena was the driver. She crashed and you covered for her."

Cody's voice was strangled to a whisper. "When we hit the tree, we were both thrown from the car. She was already dead when I found her. Killed on impact, they said. When I crawled over to her she was so ruined. I just didn't want her to suffer anymore. Her reputation was trashed by the pregnancy, she didn't need drunk driver added to her headstone. When the police showed up, it was my car so they assumed I was the driver."

"And you never corrected them?" Hannah asked incredulously.

"I loved her. You do stupid things for love."

Hannah's vision was clouded with unfathomable rage toward Elena.

Elena cheated on Cody.

Elena got pregnant by someone else.

Elena drove drunk.

Elena caused the accident.

Elena nearly killed Cody.

Elena. All of it was Elena's fault.

And Elena left Cody to deal with the fall out as if he caused it.

"Cody, who else knows this?"

"Just you," he admitted nonchalantly. "Guess that's pretty messed up, huh?"

He lifted the bottle of Jack and Hannah gently stopped it from meeting his lips.

"That's the understatement of the year," she scoffed.

Cody laughed and passed Hannah the bottle. "You look like you could use this."

"Cody, we can fix this. We need to go to the police. You've been wrongfully accused—"

"Leave it, Hannah. What's done is done."

"How can you say that? This is your life we're talking about."

"Right, *my* life."

"Well if you want to keep it a secret, fine. But I'm not living with your ghosts." Hannah got up, quickly gathering her clothes.

"Don't you dare!" Cody bellowed. "You don't get to be all high and mighty and fuck up my life just to clear your conscience."

"Look around you! It's already fucked up."

"Exactly. So just leave it alone."

"No! Not when we can fix this!"

Cody threw the bottle in frustration. "Not everything needs to be fixed, Hannah! We don't all need to be perfect like you."

Anger spiked in her heart. "I'm not perfect, Cody. But at least when I make a mistake I admit it. You have made a huge mistake and it's hurting everyone who cares about you."

"No one cares about me!"

"I do!" she screamed, her face wild with heartbreak. "I've tried so hard not to. But I care about you, Cody. And I hate that you can't see that."

Their eyes met for a fleeting moment, baring their souls. It was too much for Hannah. She needed to get out. She was suffocating from the pain that had been unleashed in Cody's room. She tried to push her way passed him but he blocked her path to the door.

His hands slid up her arms, agony painted his gorgeous face as he gently brushed Hannah's hair back, whispering her name. "I'm not worth it."

Tears burst from her eyes and she pushed him away trying for the door again.

"I'm not letting you leave like this, Hannah."

"Cody, I want to leave. I mean it."

"Not until you promise me you'll sleep on this. All of it. We can talk tomorrow. When we're not so . . . messed up."

"This will still be messed up tomorrow."

"Exactly."

"Cody, if you make me keep this secret there can never be anything between us. It'll ruin everything."

Cody shook his head, sighing with sadness. "Don't you get it. That's what I do. I ruin things. I tried to warn you."

Hannah choked back her sobs. "I wish I'd never met you."

Just then the door flew open, shoving into Cody's back pushing him into Hannah. They both stumbled back, clinging to each other to stay upright.

Harrison's face took in the scene. Hannah half naked clutching her clothes, cheeks streaked with tears. Cody shirtless and reeking of booze, his paws all over Hannah's pale skin. Harrison's rage erupted, hailing profanity and fists.

Hannah screamed, but her voice dissolved into the din of their brawling bodies.

"Stop, please stop!" she wailed as they scuffled around the room overturning everything in their path.

"She doesn't want you!" Harrison growled, leveling Cody with a punch. "Why can't you ever get that through your thick skull?"

"I know that!" Cody yelled scrambling to his feet only for Harrison to knock him into a wall.

He shoved his forearm into Cody's throat. "So you thought you'd get her drunk and force her anyway, you sick prick."

"I didn't touch her!" Cody gasped.

"I saw your hands all over her!"

"It wasn't like that."

For a moment the boys stood still, in some sort of egotistical standoff. Hannah saw her chance and pushed her way between them "Harrison. Please. He didn't hurt me. It's all a misunderstanding. I just want to go home. Can you take me home? Please?"

Harrison snapped out of his fury and recovered his composure. He let go of Cody, who crumpled to the floor like a rock. Harrison smoothed his clothes. His mouth quirked into a tight smile as he smoothed Hannah's wild hair. "You're okay?"

"Yes. Can we please go?"

"Sure. Grab your things and meet me in the car."

Hannah hesitated.

"I'm right behind you," Harrison assured her.

Hannah gave Cody a concerned look. "Are you okay?"

Cody nodded.

"I just need to discuss something with Cody, man to man. I promise. No more fighting."

Unable to fight her nerves any longer Hannah fled to the car, her sobs chasing her the whole way.

Once Harrison was sure they were alone he turned to Cody and gave him a smug grin. "You're pathetic, Matthews."

Cody didn't respond. He was busy sopping up the blood that trickled from a cut above his eye.

Harrison walked closer towering over Cody. He knelt down and handed Cody a handkerchief from his pocket. Unable to resist a final dig, Harrison leaned in so he could whisper in Cody's ear. "You never learn." Harrison laughed and patted Cody's shoulder. "I almost admire you for it. But in the end they always choose me." Harrison stood not even trying to restrain his smirk. "Hannah's mine now."

He sauntered to the door, giving Cody one last look before leaving. "You can keep the handkerchief," he called. "We'll call it a memento."

CHAPTER

35

Harrison pulled up to Hannah's. The ride home had been tense—Hannah's sobs the only sound over the engine. Once in her driveway, Hannah grabbed the door handle ready to make a quick exit. "Thank you for bringing me home."

"That's it?"

Hannah sighed. She just wanted tonight to be over. It had spiraled into some sort of bad dream. And from the way her vision blurred she wondered if maybe that's all it was. *If only she were that lucky.*

"Hannah, what were you doing at Cody's?"

"Can we talk about this tomorrow? I really don't feel well."

Harrison's jaw muscles twitched with restraint. He looked like he wanted to say something but decided against it. "Sure. Get some sleep. I'll see you tomorrow."

Relieved to finally be alone, Hannah's body sagged. She barely made it to her room before she sank to her knees. She crawled to her bathroom and threw up as sobs racked her body.

She spent most of the night curled up on her bathroom floor. Her head was spinning and her lungs couldn't seem to give her enough air. She couldn't get Cody's words out of her head. *How could he be so stupid?* He'd let his love for a dead girl ruin his life! None of it was his fault. He'd endured probation, rehab and vicious rumors . . . all for what? *To save Elena? Why would he even want to?* Elena cheated on him. She threw his love away.

Hannah's heart broke—partly for Cody and partly for herself. She'd been drunk tonight, but in the darkness of his truth, she'd found her own. She was unable to deny her feelings for Cody. Every time they'd kissed or touched her body responded in a way she couldn't explain—an explosion of desperation and completion. But none of it mattered now. The secrets between them could snuff out the fiercest of bonds, let alone a vulnerable bud of fledgling love.

Hannah dragged herself to bed, her head swimming with the events of the night. Every time she closed her eyes, she saw Cody's face—defeated and raw. No wonder he thought no one cared about him. The people who were supposed to always let him down. His parents, his girlfriend, his friends. But Hannah made up her mind, she wouldn't be another disappointment to him. Maybe he couldn't see it now, but telling the truth would set him free.

She glanced at the clock. It would be hours before she could do anything to help Cody. She pulled her pillow over her head, willing her mind to let her sleep. This mess would be waiting for her in the morning. And Hannah wanted a clear head when she told her father everything. He would know what to do.

CHAPTER
36

Cody woke with a splitting headache and a crushing ache in his chest. He'd finally shared his dark secret. But it hadn't changed a thing. If anything he'd only managed to push Hannah further away. *Good. She's safer this way,* he thought. But then he found himself wondering, *if that were true, why did it hurt so bad?*

Watching her leave with Harrison hurt worse than any of the physical blows he'd taken. He couldn't get the image out of his head. Cody took a long shower, replaying the events of the night. He wished it were as simple as washing it all down the drain. But it never was. And despite the disastrous way the night ended, Cody didn't regret it. There had been fleeting moments with Hannah that felt real. He closed his eyes, relishing the way their bodies had fit together. Mouths, hands, skin—all molded perfectly, like two halves of a singular unit. Like there was only the two of them in the world and nothing else mattered.

It had never been easy like that with Elena. They had an inevitable chemical attraction, but they'd always been fighting to fit, like magnets of opposite charge.

The water finally ran cold, pulling Cody back to reality. He exited the shower, grimacing as he gingerly patted himself dry. His whole body hurt and his face was swollen thanks to Harrison mistaking it as a punching bag. The makings of an epic shiner had already started blooming around his blood shot eye. He looked dreadful. The last time he'd seen himself so beat up was after the car accident.

Cody's mind flashed back to the gruesome memories that haunted him from the night that changed his life—Elena's broken body, the weight of her motionless in his arms, the blood. There was so much blood . . .

A wave of nausea hit Cody like a tsunami. He braced himself over the toilet and heaved. But his stomach was empty. For once, he was grateful he'd filled it with nothing but Jack.

He stared his reflection down in the mirror and found himself thinking of Hannah—wondering what she saw when she looked at him. *How had he let her get so close? To see under his carefully fabricated exterior?* A bittersweet smile twitched the corners of his lips. *Who was he kidding?* He'd never been able to fool Hannah. She'd always seen him. It was Cody who'd been blindsided. *He never saw her coming.*

He closed his eyes, letting the image of Hannah wash over him, invading his mind—quieting it with her soft features. He pictured the concern in her eyes as she hesitated to leave him last night. *She'd been worried about him.* But then Harrison stepped between them, cutting off Cody's view of the steady blue sea of Hannah's eyes. She'd been reaching out to him, offering him a lifeline to keep him afloat. And he'd pushed her away.

Clarity seized him, and Cody made a snap decision. He wasn't ready to throw in the towel just yet. Not to beat Harrison in their twisted competition that had grown from childhood rivalry into something dangerous, but for Hannah. And for any chance they might have together.

Cody dressed quickly and padded his way to the kitchen to remedy his empty stomach. The cook took one look at his bruised face and left the kitchen. The staff had seen him like this before and they knew the drill—*stay out of the way*. He threw together a sandwich and downed a coke on his way out the door.

He needed to see Hannah. They had things to discuss.

CHAPTER
37

Light knocking at Hannah's door pulled her from her slumber. Sunlight filled her bedroom. Her body caved to exhaustion and she'd slept much later than she'd intended. She sat up in bed letting the groggy veil of sleep lift from her mind.

"Hannah," her father called outside the door.

Just the person she wanted to see.

She opened the door and her face fell. Her father's features were devoid of his normal morning cheer. He looked extraordinarily upset. "Get dressed and come down stairs, please. We need to talk."

"Dad? What's wrong?"

"There's someone here to see you. I'd like you to ask him to leave, and then we need to have a serious discussion."

"Who?"

"Cody Matthews."

Hannah's heart pounded to life. "What does he want?"

"He won't say. I've asked him to leave and he's refused. I'm hoping you can talk some sense into him. If not, I'll be forced to contact the authorities."

"Dad!"

"Be quick, Hannah."

Her father closed the door and she leapt to action, throwing on her Brown sweatshirt and black leggings. She peered out the window but couldn't see Cody. No car either. He must have walked. She took a quick survey of her appearance. She looked like hell. Her eyes were puffy and the ghosts of run mascara clung beneath them. She splashed cold water on her face and did her best to rub the sleep and sorrow from her eyes.

She ran downstairs and skidded to a stop in the hall. Her father stood, arms crossed, by the front door. Through the glass Hannah could see Cody's silhouette, perched on the front steps, his shoulders slumped.

She pushed the creaking door open and Cody stood.

"Hey."

"What are you doing here?"

"I wanted to talk to you . . ." he paused and looked passed Hannah to where her father had followed her out to the porch.

She turned to him. "Dad. Can I have a moment alone to speak with Cody?"

Her father spoke in hushed tones. "I don't like this, Hannah. He looks like he's been in brawl. I'm not comfortable leaving you alone with him."

"Please, Dad. Just go inside. You can keep you eye on us the whole time."

"Five minutes, Hannah. And then I want him gone. I mean it."

Hannah waited until her father was inside, the door shut firmly behind him before walking over to Cody. She took his hand and walked him down the stairs away from the porch. She trudged silently through the spring grass to her old swing set. A skeleton of her youth, it sat rusting in the rose garden a few yards from the house. It was in perfect view of the large picture window in the living room, where Hannah was sure her father would be watching, but it would ensure their conversation wouldn't be overheard.

Hannah perched on a swing and nodded for Cody to do the same.

"Why are you here?"

"I wanted to apologize for last night."

"You said that already."

Cody looked down at his shoes, scuffing them into the soft earth.

"We have five minutes until my dad calls the police so I'd advise you to say whatever you came to say and then leave."

Cody's head jerked up. He stared into Hannah's eyes and she held his gaze. "Don't go to the party tonight, Hannah."

She laughed.

"I'm serious. I have a bad feeling about it. I don't want to see you get hurt."

"A little late for that, don't you think?"

"I never meant to hurt you, Hannah."

"If that's all, I think you should leave," Hannah said standing.

Cody stood too and took her hands pleadingly. "Please, Hannah. If you're set on going let me go with you."

"I'm going with Harrison."

"He's playing a game, Hannah, and it's not going to end well."

"Not everything is a game. I think Harrison actually cares about me."

"You're too smart to be that stupid, Hannah."

Hannah ripped her hands from Cody's. "I see. Just because you don't want me, no one does?"

"No! That's not what I'm saying."

"Then tell me, Cody. What *are* you saying?"

"I don't know. I can't explain it, but I know Harrison's using you."

Tears stung her eyes, but she refused to cry in front of him. "Of course," she whispered. "Because it's unthinkable that someone could actually fall for me."

"Hannah—"

"Leave me alone, Cody." She turned to leave, but he blocked her path.

"Fine. Keep my secret about Elena and you'll never see me again."

"I'm not making any promises. I don't owe you anything."

The front door opened and Hannah's father walked onto the porch. His face looking like a tea kettle about to whistle. She fled back toward her house, straight into his arms. She let him fold her up like a frightened child, while he glared at Cody, who wisely kept his head down and walked down the driveway and out of their lives.

~♡~

The walk home was long for Cody. The weather had

turned agreeable and the sunshine and birdsongs only worsened his mood. He scowled as the world around him went merrily on while leaving him in the same insufferable spot—alone.

At least he'd tried with Hannah.

True, he hadn't exactly had a chance to share his feelings, but there was nothing more to do. He'd screwed up again. He knew a lost cause when he saw one. *He looked in the mirror often enough.*

CHAPTER

38

Hannah's father held her tight. He stroked her hair like he used to when she was a child. He'd calmly held her hand while she spilled her guts about the last few weeks with Cody and Harrison. She told him everything, even the unflattering things. The lies, the drinking, the blackmail and upcoming party. But mostly she told him about Cody. She confided her fleeting feelings for him and her abrupt heartbreak over the gravity of his secrets and what really happened with Elena.

"What am I going to do?"

"Hannah, I'm sorry you're going through all of this. I know growing up is inevitable, but sometimes I fear I may have sheltered you from the world too well."

"Dad, this isn't your fault."

"I know." He sighed. "I'm not happy about some of your decisions, but I am grateful that you were brave enough to tell me. I want you to know you can always trust me, baby."

"I know, Dad." Hannah hugged her father tighter. "But what do we do for Cody?"

"Honestly, I don't know, Hannah. It's not easy to help someone who doesn't want to be helped."

Hannah saw the pain in her father's eyes and knew he was thinking of her mother.

"But I can't do nothing. It's wrong to keep this all bottled up. I think it will haunt me."

"Let me think on it for a bit. I have some friends I can ask for legal advice."

"How long will that take?"

"Hannah, you need to understand this isn't something we can fix overnight."

"I know, but I feel like I'm going crazy just sitting here doing nothing."

Her father exhaled slowly. "I can't believe I'm going to say this but do you still want to go to the party tonight?"

"You'll let me go?"

"Do you still want to go?"

"Yes. I know this didn't start out right, but I think I actually might like Harrison."

"Do you feel you can trust him and make responsible decisions?"

"Yes."

"And Cody won't be there?"

"No."

"Then I think a distraction might be the best thing for you."

Hannah squealed and hugged her father tight.

"But I want to know where you are, who you're with and you're to be home by ten."

"Dad, the party doesn't start until ten!"

He grumbled something under his breath about kids these days. "Fine, midnight. But you're to text me every hour."

"I will."

"I mean it. I'm not above showing up there if you're late."

"I love you, Dad," Hannah said kissing him on the cheek.

"I love you, too."

Hannah retrieved her borrowed dress from her car, which had been safely returned as promised. There was even a delicate black mask in the bottom of the garment bag. Hannah grabbed her phone and sent Savannah a quick text to thank her.

STILL COMING TONIGHT – SAVANNAH

YES – HANNAH

IMPRESSED.
HEARD H & C GOT INTO IT LAST NIGHT
– SAVANNAH

Hannah sighed. *Of course the gossip was already swirling.* She was honestly impressed with the way the student body at Stanton kept their fingers on the pulse of peril. It was like they could smell drama.

DEETS – SAVANNAH

ALL GOOD.
FILL U IN TONIGHT – HANNAH

U BETTER – SAVANNAH

Hannah clicked off her phone and put it on the charger. It was about dead after being left in her car all night. She headed to the shower and turned her attention to getting ready for her first and last high school party.

CHAPTER
39

DID U REALLY DRUG HANNAH – SAVANNAH

Cody glared at his phone. It had been going off all afternoon. He was doing his best to ignore it but Savannah and her minions, wouldn't leave him alone.

THAT'S A NEW LOW. EVEN FOR U.
NO RESPONSE FROM THE GUILTY.
WONDER WHAT HANNAH WILL SAY?
I TOLD HER NOT TO GO TO YOUR PLACE LAST NIGHT.
BUT SHE BEGGED AND BEGGED – SAVANNAH

U BROUGHT HER HERE – CODY

SHE LOVES U.
I SAW IT IN HER PATHETIC FACE.

YOU'RE SUCH A HEARTBREAKER – SAVANNAH

LEAVE HER ALONE – CODY

YOU FIRST – SAVANNAH

DO U GET OFF ON THIS – CODY

GUESS U HAVEN'T SEEN FB?
IT'S NOT JUST ME – SAVANNAH

Cody flipped open his laptop and pulled up the secret Stanton group everyone used to post the most gruesome gossip. His stomach dropped when he saw Hannah's name lighting up the feed. She had a private social profile so no one could tag her, but that almost made it worse because people where using her first and last name. The theme of the defaming posts were mostly against Cody. Claiming he got Hannah drunk and laced her drinks with drugs so he could take advantage of her. Harrison was of course cast as the hero, swooping in and saving Hannah. And beating Cody to a pulp.

A dark picture began to work its way into Cody's mind. Savannah had always been a jealous bitch. She'd caused trouble for him and Elena in the past. And it was a little too convenient that she brought Hannah to Cody's house last night and Harrison just happened to show up. Then there was the way Hannah had been acting. She'd admitted to drinking some champagne but everything about her manner seemed off—over stimulated. Had he not been so drunk himself, Cody would have seen it sooner. Hannah was high. He didn't know on what, but he'd been to enough of Savannah's parties over the years to know she loved to play pharmacist, mixing up her own special *'candy'* as she called it.

Cody's blood pressure soared. He stormed into his closet and grabbed his tux. He was through letting the Goldens ruin people's lives. He was more certain than ever that something twisted was about to go down at Harrison's party and there was no way he was letting Hannah walk into it alone.

CHAPTER

40

Hannah checked the address she'd been texted for what felt like the hundredth time. The location of the party was only revealed a few hours before it started, per Cohl tradition. The whole family certainly had a flare for the dramatic. It wasn't that surprising to hear the party would be hosted at the Cohl country manor house, but after driving down a wooded dirt road for nearly twenty minutes Hannah began to feel her skin prickle. And she wasn't sure whether it was from nervous excitement to see Harrison or something more sinister. She'd never been comfortable with the idea of being far from civilization. That was always where things went wrong . . . well at least in all the books she'd read.

The GPS alerted her to turn off the dirt road onto what could only be described as a path. She'd almost decided to turn back when she came to a massive iron gate. It was wide open, inviting her in. And in the distance she could see lights.

She drove through the gate and ventured a little further up the path. The trees finally gave way, opening up to reveal a gorgeous two-story colonial brick home, complete with white pillars and climbing ivy. It was right out of a storybook. Well, except for the bumping base that spilled across the immaculate lawn that now resembled a car park.

She was in the right place all right.

Hannah drove across a small bridge and around the circle drive, where her car was valeted. She walked up the polished flagstone steps and stared at the black menacing double doors. There was no one to greet her and when she tried the handle it was locked. Immediate panic flooded her heart.

Had she been lured out her as a joke?

But then she remembered—the key.

Hannah pulled it from her tiny black clutch and nervously slid it into the keyhole. She closed her eyes and offered up a silent prayer before turning it. A faint *click* echoed around her and the door swung open, ushering her into another world.

So this was a Cohl Ball?

A feeling of Alice discovering Wonderland overtook Hannah. She could immediately see the allure. She felt like she'd been whisked into a secret world that only the rich and beautiful were privy to. Masked figures in exquisite gowns and tuxedos dotted the black and white checkered floors. Their whispers and laughter rose above the scratchy wail of '20s Parisian music while they indulged themselves in cocktails, music and the unparalleled pleasures the Cohl Manor offered. The scene was a strange mix of Gatsby and Eyes Wide Shut.

A twinge of panic gripped Hannah as she glanced around for familiar faces.

How would she ever find anyone among the sea of masks?

She was about to start wandering from room to room looking for Harrison when she heard his voice. She looked up and saw him gallantly descending the grand staircase. His charming smile disarmed her. It was dazzlingly white in contrast to his dark mask.

He took Hannah's hand and bowed, brushing his lips against her knuckles. Blissful excitement raced to her heart.

"You look ravishing," he murmured spinning her around to take in the full beauty of her shimmering silver sheath gown. It was simple, but its barely-there spaghetti straps and open back made it feel daring.

Hannah giggled, feeling ridiculously girly as she allowed Harrison to pull her into his arms and give her a chaste kiss.

"I'm so glad you came. I was worried that you wouldn't after last night."

"Me too," Hannah admitted. "Turns out my dad thinks I need a distraction."

Harrison smirked. "I like the way he thinks." He kissed Hannah again, leaving her breathless. "Well now that you're here. The party can start." He took her hand. "Come on," he urged. "Let's get you a drink."

"Oh I promised no drinking tonight."

Harrison winked. "I won't tell if you won't."

He didn't give Hannah a chance to protest, leading her through rooms of intoxicating grandeur, stopping to make small talk when necessary. They entered a small room that glowed with soft blue light. The music was weaker and masked figures lazed about, draped over low-backed couches and upholstered chairs. Some were indulging in each other, while others just seemed to be staring into space. The scene reminded Hannah of the opium dens she'd read about. And one glance at the bar explained why. It held more than liquor bottles. A gilded sign, donning it the 'Candy Bar' gleamed back at Hannah as her eyes raked over martini glasses full of pills and powders of varying colors.

Harrison made his way back from the bar with two glasses in his hands. He handed Hannah the champagne flute, while keeping the rocks glass with swirling amber liquid for himself.

"Oh I really think I better not. I had enough of this last night."

"Would you like something else?" Harrison asked, a hint of something sinister in his voice.

Hannah was beginning to hate the masks. It made it impossible to read Harrison's features and that made her edgy. "Maybe a water?"

Harrison glanced back at the bar and frowned. "I didn't think to stock the bar with water."

"Oh, that's fine. I'm not really that thirsty," Hannah said trying to hand the glass back to Harrison.

"I thought you wanted a fun distraction tonight?" Harrison asked.

"I do."

He grinned. "Good. Then hang onto the champagne. You might get thirsty," he said extending his arm to Hannah.

She threaded her arm through his, just wanting to leave the hedonistic room behind.

"Come on," Harrison said. "I want to give you the tour."

CHAPTER

41

Cody steeled himself as he walked up to the front door of the Cohl manor.

Of course this was where the party was.

The last time Cody had been there was the night Elena died. Tonight's drive had been a battle of wills for Cody as he barreled down the dark roads that haunted his memories. The only thing that kept him going was Hannah, and his need to protect her from whatever cruel game the Goldens were playing.

He tried his key in the door and breathed a sigh of relief when the lock tumbled granting him entrance. Cody walked into his own personal hell. Memories exploded like flash bulbs in his mind has he desperately fought to breathe through the crushing pain in his chest. He'd had so many good times at this house with Elena, Harrison and the Goldens. But all of that was erased in one night, and an indelible darkness was left on his soul.

A shrill voice broke Cody from his nightmare.

"Well look who it is?"

He looked up to see Savannah sneering at him under her frilly pink mask.

"You must be confused, we scheduled the trash pick up for tomorrow, Cody."

Cody was wearing a classic tux and plain black mask. He looked identical to every other guy at the party, but he'd been foolish to think he'd slip by unnoticed. Savannah had a sixth sense for sniffing out weaknesses to exploit. She'd locked onto him like a bloodhound.

"Unless you have some dogs to run over I think you should leave," she hissed.

Cody snapped and grabbed Savannah by the arm eliciting a shriek from her.

"I'd be happy too, but not without Hannah."

"Didn't get enough of her last night?"

"What's your role in this?"

"I don't know what you're talking about."

"Cut the shit, Savannah. I know you're the one who got Hannah drunk and high and sent her to my house last night. Just what the hell did you think was going to happen?"

"You tell me. You're the murdering drunk."

"So that's your game. You want her out of your way?"

"You said it, not me," Savannah hissed.

"Do you really think you're never going to get caught? One time you're going to go too far and someone's going to OD."

"I can only hope," Savannah grinned.

Cody's grip tightened and her smile dissolved.

"Oh calm down. It was just a little harmless candy. If you ask me I did her a favor. She's way too uptight."

Cody took a steadying breath, telling himself to walk away because Savannah was wearing his already thin nerves to nothing and all he wanted to do was knock her pearly veneers down her throat. "Just tell me where she is."

Savannah shrugged. "Haven't seen her, sorry." She slipped around Cody and slithered away to rejoin the party.

Cody ripped off his mask in frustration. There was no sense hiding now. If Savannah knew he was here, soon everyone would. Maybe that was good. Maybe it would flush Harrison out quicker and he could find Hannah and get the hell out.

CHAPTER

42

Hannah found herself in the eight-bay carriage house that had been converted into a garage to house the Cohl's precious collection of luxury cars. She rather enjoyed the manor tour so far, marveling at the amazing artwork and décor. Her favorite area had been the back garden, where she'd strategically dumped her champagne without Harrison noticing.

She found herself grateful to be away from the suffocating atmosphere of the party. It was funny how badly she'd wanted to attend and pretend she was part of the in-crowd. But now that she was here . . . she just wanted to leave. It was clear this lifestyle wasn't for her. Harrison was handsome and flattering. He said all the right things and knew exactly how to make her swoon with subtle touches and kisses. But something was missing.

Her inner goddess berated her. *Who wouldn't want a guy like Harrison?*

Hannah fully admitted she'd begun to fall for him when

they'd been on their whirlwind yachting date. It was easy to get carried away imagining an adventurous life sailing to exotic places. But something in the back of her practical mind warned her that none of it was true. And it wasn't what she wanted. She wanted more.

Who has more than Harrison Cohl? her inner goddess chided.

But that wasn't the kind of *more* she meant.

More connection.

More depth.

More reciprocation.

Hannah realized that she'd been blinded by Harrison's flashiness. And when all of his extravagance was stripped away, there was nothing left.

She found herself thinking of all the discussions she'd had with Cody over the past few weeks. How he'd asked her a million questions about herself. Many were embarrassing, but he'd genuinely wanted to know about her. Harrison rarely asked Hannah any questions, except if she wanted more champagne. He'd spent the entire night boasting about himself.

"This one's my favorite," Harrison announced, bringing Hannah back to the present.

They stood in front of an old-fashioned car. Its dove gray, high-gloss finish was polished to a sheen that displayed Hannah's reflection back to her with near perfection.

"1934 Rolls-Royce Phantom II Kellner Cariolet."

Hannah smiled, though the words meant nothing to her.

"Father says it's mine when I graduate."

"It's lovely."

"Not as lovely as you," Harrison purred, untying the ribbon on Hannah's mask.

He pulled it from her face and leaned in to kiss her but Hannah turned her cheek. The evening had suddenly lost its sparkle after her sullen realization that Harrison was not the guy for her.

Unfazed by her dismissive move, Harrison kissed Hannah's neck, sending her senses into a tizzy that warred with her mind. He pulled off his own mask and clicked open the car door. "Wanna go for a test drive?"

"Um, actually I think I'm going to head home."

"You just got here. The fun hasn't even started yet."

There was a dangerous current to the way Harrison was looking at her now.

"I told my dad I wouldn't be out late, so—"

"Come on, go for a ride with me, Hannah. We can pretend it's graduation night. I want to make sure we have enough room to celebrate properly."

Hannah's stomach dropped at his less than subtle innuendo.

"I really need to be going."

Harrison's hand firmly encircled Hannah's waist locking her in place. "Do you want me to beg? I've been told I can be very convincing."

"Harrison . . ."

"Get in the car, Hannah."

"Please—"

The rest of Hannah's words were swallowed by the roughness of Harrison's mouth on hers as he shoved her into the car. His powerful body pinned her to the leather while his hands harshly roamed her body, yanking her thin straps down.

"Stop!" Hannah cried out over and over but Harrison only laughed.

"Oh you're going to be fun."

CHAPTER

43

Cody's heart was pounding by the time he spilled out the backdoor of the Cohl manor. He'd gotten sick of waiting around and took matters into his own hands. He turned the house upside down looking for Hannah. All the while ignoring the whispers and stares he encountered in every room.

There was no sign of her.

He drank in the cool night air, scanning his surroundings. *Where the hell were they?*

Cody's eyes rested on the carriage house. He and Harrison used to sneak in there when they were younger to smoke weed. He remembered getting caught by the housekeeper. She threw a fit—the carriage house was off limits.

It was the perfect place to hide.

Cody's nerves sizzled as he moved toward the carriage house with purpose. He could see the light filter through the windowpanes in the door.

Someone was in there.

Something in his gut told him to run. He was breathless when he reached the door but it was locked. He jiggled the handle hard calling Hannah's name. It didn't budge. He even rammed his shoulder into it with no results.

He ran around front to the keypad and prayed the code was still the same.

As he rounded the front of the carriage house his knees went weak. *It happened right here.* This was where he and Elena had their final fight. He pictured her beautiful face, tortured with hurt as she slung accusations at him. Her voice echoed in his mind. *'Nothing will ever be the same.'*

She was right. Nothing was the same after that night.

Cody doubled over, cutting his hands as he caught himself in the gravel of the driveway. He heaved up his dinner and let the tears come, wondering how the hell he'd ended up back here after all this time.

CHAPTER
44

"You're just like her you know," Harrison goaded, stroking Hannah's hair as she flailed beneath him. "Not the hair of course, but the eyes and feistiness. Cody certainly has a type."

Hannah's heart iced over. "Oh my god." She stopped fighting and stared up at Harrison. "It was you. You're the one Elena was cheating on Cody with."

"Ever the little genius, aren't you, Hannah?"

"You disgusting pig! Did you force her too?"

Harrison grinned. "Come now, you know you want me."

"Is that what you told Elena?"

Anger dissolved Harrison's smug exterior. He glared at Hannah, gripping her wrists tighter. "I didn't have to. The little slut begged for it. She was frustrated and needy, so disappointed that her sweet boyfriend wanted to wait. I gave her what she wanted." He laughed. "Right in this very car, actually."

"Get off of me!" Hannah screamed trying uselessly to fight Harrison's solid body off of her.

"I did learn my lesson about protection though," he said holding up a condom.

"Cody will kill you when he finds out."

"I doubt that. Especially once I show him our little flick." Harrison gestured over his shoulder to a blinking red light mounted on the seatback. "Did you know I'm studying film at Harvard next year? It's incredible what you can do with editing programs these days."

"You'll never get away with this," she sobbed as his hands slithered under her dress.

"Sure I will, Hannah. I always do."

Hannah closed her eyes and screamed as loud as she could, but she knew it was useless. Harrison would win. He always did.

CHAPTER
45

A scream ripped Cody from his darkness. It was Hannah. He knew it surer than he knew his own name. He scrambled to his feet, screaming her name.

"Hannah!"

Cody found the keypad and punched in the code with shaking fingers—Harrison's birthday. He'd always been his parents' favorite.

Relief flooded him when the door softly groaned open.

"Hannah!"

Her voice rang out clear as day. "Cody! Help!"

He ran toward her voice through the maze of cars. Rage nearly blinded him when he spotted her—Harrison pinning her in the back of his Royce.

❧

One minute Harrison's weight was crushing Hannah and the next he was gone. He disappeared as if sucked through the fuselage of an unpressurized aircraft. Cody's furious voice filled the air as he slammed Harrison onto the hood of the car.

"You piece of shit," Cody screamed as he pummeled Harrison's face. "I'll kill you if you hurt her. Do you hear me? I'll kill you." Cody rained down punch after punch into Harrison's face until blood was pouring from his nose and mouth. "Don't you ever touch her again!" Cody growled, slamming Harrison into the hood of the priceless car with disgust.

His initial fury drained, Cody turned his attention to Hannah. "Are you okay?" he asked softly. But Hannah didn't get to reply.

Harrison dove onto Cody. "She wanted it," he screamed as he swung at Cody. "All your girls want me!"

"Shut up!" Cody scathed landing a sickening punch to Harrison's face.

Harrison spit blood and smiled before slamming his head into Cody's face.

The battle had begun.

Hannah righted her dress and tried to crawl from the car but was knocked back in by the war that was raging in the garage. She had a front row seat as Harrison and Cody wrestled each other to the ground, punching and kicking.

This fight had been brewing for ages and all Hannah could do was sit by and watch, trying to not become a casualty.

"I love how easy your girls are," Harrison jeered unable to resist taking verbal jabs at Cody as well as physical. "They're all backseat sluts. Hannah couldn't resist anymore than Elena could."

Cody's face turned white and Harrison took advantage of his shock, throwing Cody off of him and getting to his feet.

Harrison circled Cody with predatorily focus.

Get up! Hannah willed as she watched the scene unfold. *Get up!*

But Cody didn't get up. He stayed on his knees, blood dripping from his face. He looked up at Harrison with more hurt than Hannah had ever seen.

"I always knew it was you." Cody's stunned voice was barely above a whisper.

"The truth hurts doesn't it?" Harrison mocked.

"Why?" Cody yelled finding his voice again and climbing to his feet.

"Who cares? Just admit that you've lost and get the fuck out of my life!"

"What the hell did I ever do to you, Harrison?"

"You were born." Harrison screamed, the vein in his neck looking like it was going to burst. "You are what's wrong with me! Your existence is a constant reminder of my ruined family and I won't stop until I've destroyed you, the way your mother destroyed us."

"What are you talking about?"

Harrison cocked his head, puzzled. Then he unleashed hysterical laughter. "You really don't know, do you?"

"Enlighten me."

"This is too good to be true." Harrison clasped his hands behind his back and paced like a professor giving a lecture. "Where to start, where to start. Ah, how about at the beginning, dear brother?"

Cody looked like a fighter about to go down. He wobbled on his legs and Harrison caught him. He wasn't done toying with him yet.

"That's right," Harrison hissed. "Haven't you ever wondered why our parents divorced the same year? Or why my father's always been so kind to you? Even going as far as to have his legal team represent you to get your sentence reduced? It should have been manslaughter, but Daddy couldn't let his youngest end up in prison, could he?"

Cody shoved Harrison off him. "You're lying!"

"I wish. But your whore of a mother couldn't keep her legs closed around my father. God knows how she lured him to bed. Probably got him drunk. Alcohol has always been the choice weapon in your family."

"Don't talk about my mother!"

"Why? She never wanted you. She wanted my father. You were just a misfortunate byproduct of their affair."

Cody staggered back from Harrison's cutting words. Shock and disbelief warred on his face.

Hannah couldn't take anymore of this nightmare. She slipped from the backseat of the car and edged her way toward Cody, slipping her hand into his. He looked at her, momentarily dazed, like he'd forgotten she was even there.

"Come on. Let's go," Hannah begged pulling Cody toward the open garage door.

"Think about it, Cody," Harrison called. "Deep down you've always known it's true."

Hannah tugged relentlessly at Cody's arm, making progress one foot at a time. They were almost out of the garage. Cool air brushed her skin with the promise of freedom, but Harrison wouldn't stop. He just kept taunting.

"Too bad everyone always chooses me," Harrison goaded.

"Elena, Hannah, our Father. He knew the truth about Elena, ya know? He knew I got her pregnant, but he wasn't going to let my record be tarnished. That's why he let you take the fall. You're illegitimate and you always will be."

"What's to stop me from going to the police about this?" Cody snarled as Hannah clung to his arm, holding him from falling to pieces.

Harrison laughed. "Like anyone would believe you."

Hannah had enough. She'd tried to stay quiet, but this was too much. She spoke in a deadly calm voice staring directly at Harrison. "But they might believe me."

"That's sweet. But you don't have any proof."

Hannah slowly reached into her black clutch and pulled out the camera she'd stolen from the back seat of Harrison's car.

His eyes widened and his nostrils flared with hatred. "You little bitch."

"Run," Cody yelled, pushing Hannah out the garage door.

She heard him scuffling with Harrison behind her as she ran as fast as she could toward the house. The sound of gravel crunching behind her made her turn. Cody sprinted after her. But just steps behind him was Harrison.

"Keys," Cody shouted, throwing them at her. "Get to my car and get out of here."

She caught them and nodded, not hesitating for a second. She spotted Cody's Range Rover parked in front of the manor. She got in and started it up. The seat remembered her, boosting her forward as she pushed the clutch into drive, speeding back toward the garage.

Cody and Harrison were rolling around in the gravel trying to kill each other. Hannah laid on the horn and skidded to a stop as close to them as she dared. It had the desired effect. Both boys separated, launching themselves out of the way thinking she was going to run them over. Cody jumped into the car and Hannah hit the lock button, leaving Harrison chasing after them as they sped off into the wild wooded darkness.

CHAPTER

46

Hannah careened down the driveway and out the gate, fishtailing wildly on the soft dirt road. Cody was breathing hard, his arms cradling his head as he rocked dangerously close to the dash.

"I think I'm going to be sick," he mumbled.

"Just breathe, Cody. I'm right here," Hannah murmured.

She wanted to rub his back soothingly but she didn't dare take her hands off the wheel. She was driving at a breakneck pace and each bump threatened to send them hurtling toward the trees.

"Those things he said . . . it's all true isn't it? He's my brother. He got Elena pregnant. And his father . . . our father covered it up?"

"It's not all true, Cody."

"What part?"

"The part about everyone choosing him. I didn't choose him. I'm choosing you."

Cody looked at her for the first time. His face was a bloody mess but he smiled ruefully, reaching his hand over to take hers. They laced their fingers together and squeezed. "Thank you," he whispered.

They finally reached the main road, but Hannah still didn't feel safe. She glanced in her rearview mirror repeatedly, expecting to see Harrison tailing them.

"Where to?" she asked.

Cody laughed. "I don't know. Where do you go after learning your life has been one big lie?"

Hannah squeezed his hand affectionately. "I know just the place."

⁓

Hannah pulled up to the grassy ridge overlooking the stables. It was almost more beautiful at night. The frantic pounding of her heart finally began to slow. There was nothing around them for miles. They would be safe here. She looked over at Cody. His eyes were closed tightly, as if he was wrestling heavy demons.

"Wanna get some fresh air?" she asked.

He opened his eyes and visibly relaxed once he realized where they were. "I like your choice of location."

"Someone once told me this place makes everything better."

Cody tried to smile. "At least some things are still true."

"Come on, let's get some air."

They exited the car and walked to the front, leaning back against the warmth of the grill.

"The stars look beautiful from here," Hannah remarked.

Cody remained silent, staring off into the distance.

"Nothing has to change unless you want it to," Hannah whispered, slipping her hand into Cody's.

He wrapped his arms around her and pulled her in tight. "But I want things to change. I want this . . . us . . . to be real," he said with resolve.

Hannah gazed up at him, watching the starlight that danced across his dark eyes. His face was bruised and bloodied, but he'd never looked more beautiful to her. Cody inched his face closer to hers, his breath catching when it mixed with hers.

"I do too," she whispered, stretching to her toes, closing the distance until their lips touched.

For a moment the world stood still. Her lips on his— breathing as one. And then they let go and lost each other in a kiss that transcended all others. It spoke of undeclared love and compassion, and longing. It promised trust and faithfulness. And above all, it was pure—untainted with any motive other than their hearts' honest desire for each other.

When they pulled away they were breathless. It was Hannah who spoke first.

"Cody, I want to be here for you. Whatever decision you make, I'll stand by you."

"I don't know what to do, Hannah. But I can't live with all these lies anymore. It's killing me."

"Then let it out."

"How?"

"I have the video. I got Harrison's whole confession on camera."

"How did you manage that?"

"You don't want to know."

"I don't want any secrets between us," Cody pleaded, gently tucking back a stray hair from Hannah's face.

"Harrison set up a camera in the car. He planned to record his conquest," she said softly.

"Hannah? Did he hurt you? Because I swear—"

"No. But I think he would have if you hadn't shown up when you did."

Cody's hands shook as he placed them on either side of Hannah's face letting his forehead rest against hers. The anguish on his face was excruciating. His whole body trembled with the strain of the night.

"It's okay," Hannah soothed gently trailing kisses over his cheeks and eyelids. "Everything's going to be okay."

"Hannah, if I lost you . . ."

"Shhh . . . I'm right here, Cody."

He opened his eyes and looked at her. "Tell me what to do. How do I fix this?"

"I say we share the video. Now, before Harrison has time to cover it up."

"But . . . what about you. You're on the video too."

She nodded.

"I don't want to drag you into my messed up life."

"I think it's too late for that," she smiled running her hand through his hair affectionately.

"True." He sighed. "So you really think I should do this?"

"Yes."

"Now?"

"I think the best thing you can do right now is follow the rules."

"Rules?"

Hannah smiled shyly. "A very wise man once taught me three important rules to success. Be truthful. Do what I say without question. And work quickly."

Cody laughed for the first time since they arrived. It was good to hear the familiar sound. "You know I was really just winging it, right?"

"Turns out you were pretty spot on," Hannah replied. "Listen Cody, the decision has to be yours, but if you want to do something about this I think it has to be now. Or you run the risk of Harrison covering his tracks."

Cody's jaw twitched with apprehension, but he nodded. "You're right."

Hannah opened her clutch and pulled out the tiny camera.

"Are you sure about this?" Cody asked.

"Cody . . . I'm all in."

He kissed her forehead and took the camera, adeptly connecting the Bluetooth to his phone. He uploaded the video to the Stanton student page and stared at the file for a long time. It was eleven minutes and thirty-six seconds long. That was the time it would take to change his life forever.

"I don't think I can press *post*." Cody handed the camera to Hannah. "Can you do it?"

"Let's do it together," she offered.

They climbed up onto the hood of Cody's car. Hannah shivered in her tattered dress and Cody draped his tuxedo jacket over her shoulders. Then, they linked hands and pressed *post*.

CHAPTER
47

Hannah and Cody lay back against the windshield, snuggled in each other's arms staring at the sky. Once the video went live, Cody's phone exploded to life. He switched it off and kissed Hannah softly, gazing into her eyes. "I guess you were right."

"About what?"

"Practice does make perfect."

Hannah laughed, leaning into his kiss. "We're far from perfect."

"I can live with that."

"Me too."

EPILOGUE

An official investigation was opened after Hannah's video caught the attention of law officials. It turned out everything Harrison said was true. Well everything except for the fact that he always won. This time he lost. And he lost big time.

Harrison and his father were both convicted of fraud and sentenced to prison. The investigation revealed even larger cover-ups in the Cohl family. And Mr. Cohl was indicted on several charges.

Cody's record was expunged and he received a huge settlement from the state for being wrongfully accused.

After graduation—where Hannah gave an epic speech about leaving juvenile pettiness behind to forge a new path into a future open with possibilities to become your best self—Hannah and Cody took his settlement check and chartered a sailboat for a month long adventure. Just the two of them, Custard and the sea.

And a world of infinite possibility.

THE
END

To my readers,

I want to personally thank you for taking the time to seek out this great little indie book. Writing is truly my passion. I believe each of us can find a small part of ourselves in every book we read, and carry it with us, shaping our world, our adventures and our dreams.

Following my dream to write frees my soul but knowing others find joy in my writing is indescribable. So thank you for your support and I hope your enjoyed your brief escape into the magic of these pages.

If you enjoyed this story, don't worry, there's plenty more currently rattling around in my rambunctious imagination. Let me and others know your thoughts by sharing a review of this book. Reviews help shape my next writing projects. So if you want more books like this one be sure to shout it from the rooftops (or social media.) ;-)

ABOUT THE AUTHOR

Award-Winning author, Christina Benjamin, lives in Florida with her husband, and character inspiring pets, where she spends her free time working on her books and speaking to inspire fellow writers.

Christina is best known for her wildly popular Young Adult series, The Geneva Project.

Her best-selling novel, The Geneva Project - Truth, has won multiple awards and stolen the hearts of YA readers. Packed with magic and imagination, her epic tale of adventure hooks fans of mega-hit YA fiction like Harry Potter, The Hunger Games and Percy Jackson.

Christina loves to read and write across genres. YA is her favorite but she's a sucker for a good love story. Don't miss her romance, paranormal and historical fiction, as well as the multiple anthologies she's been a part of.

To learn about new books and more fun stuff, follow her at:
FACEBOOK
@ChristinaBenjaminAuthor

TWITTER
@authorcbenjamin

INSTAGRAM
@authorcbenjamin

PINTEREST
@authorcbenjamin

WEBSITE
www.christinabenjaminauthor.com

Made in the USA
Middletown, DE
14 February 2019